THE CAPTIVE

Center Point
Large Print

Also by Carter Travis Young and available from Center Point Large Print:

Guns of Darkness
Winter of the Coup

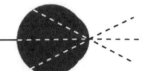

**This Large Print Book carries the
Seal of Approval of N.A.V.H.**

THE CAPTIVE

by
Carter Travis Young

CENTER POINT LARGE PRINT
THORNDIKE, MAINE

This Center Point Large Print edition
is published in the year 2019 by arrangement with
Golden West Literary Agency.

Originally published in the US by Doubleday.

The text of this Large Print edition is unabridged.
In other aspects, this book may vary
from the original edition.
Printed in the United States of America
on permanent paper.
Set in 16-point Times New Roman type.

ISBN: 978-1-64358-271-9 (hardcover)
ISBN: 978-1-64358-275-7 (paperback)

Library of Congress Cataloging-in-Publication Data

Names: Young, Carter Travis, author.
Title: The captive / Carter Travis Young.
Description: Center Point Large Print edition. | Thorndike, Maine :
    Center Point Large Print, 2019.
Identifiers: LCCN 2019017948| ISBN 9781643582719 (hardcover :
    alk. paper) | ISBN 9781643582757 (paperback : alk. paper)
Subjects: LCSH: Large type books. | GSAFD: Western stories.
Classification: LCC PS3575.O7 C3 2019 | DDC 813/.54—dc23
LC record available at https://lccn.loc.gov/2019017948

Author's Note

The central characters and their actions in this novel are fictional. The western world in which their adventure takes place, however, is as accurate historically as it was possible for me to make it, including the larger events that provide a framework for the action of the story. The authentic characters who move in and out of the story are true in their time and place. Irish Tom Fitzpatrick, Uncle Dick Wootton, and Old Bill Williams were on the scene then, and quite capable of the actions attributed to them. William Bent was at Bent's Fort that summer, his partner having gone to St. Louis with the company's caravan as described. Lieutenant John Love of the United States Army, whose fortuitous appearance along the trail from Santa Fe to Bent's Fort interrupts a Comanche attack, was, in fact, traveling that route with his dragoons at the time. Lieutenant Colonel William Gilpin's Indian Battalion undertook the punitive expedition described in the spring of 1848, the participation of Ter Bryant and Long Tom Brock being the added fictional element.

Although it is impossible to list all of those to whom I am indebted for the inspiration and background of this story, I would like to mention a few books that were especially helpful. These include: David Lavender's *Bent's Fort*; Bernard De Voto's *The Year of Decision: 1846* and *Across the Wide Missouri*; George Bird Grinnell's *The Fighting Cheyennes*; Paul Horgan's *The Heroic Triad*; Robert Glass Cleland's *This Reckless Breed of Men*; Don Berry's *A Majority of Scoundrels*; Josiah Gregg's *The Commerce of the Prairies*; and Carl P. Russell's *Firearms, Traps and Tools of the Mountain Men*. There are, of course, countless other pioneers along this trail to whom we are all gratefully indebted.

1 / Death in the Mountains

ONE

Death was his way of life. He could sense its presence even before it showed itself. For nearly a score of years he had lived by killing. Beaver for their plews. Deer and elk and buffalo for their meat and their hides. And, if need be, two-legged creatures of his own kind, white or red. He knew all the ways of killing, and his powerful rawboned body bore a hundred scars from his close scrapes with the demon. Death—his own or another's—could no longer move him.

Wo-Man was dying. Angus Haws, standing near the exit flaps of the tipi, looked down at her. A small pyramid of twigs and cut branches burned in the fire pit near the center of the lodge, directly under the smoke flaps. By its feeble light he saw the knowledge of death in her eyes.

He felt a nudge of surprise, that was all. The night before she had been hot with the fever, unable to keep food on her stomach. In the darkness of night he had wakened several times to hear her hoarse breathing. But he had known such fevers himself and shrugged them off. If he

7

had expected anything at all, it was that the fever would break, either during the night or in the next day or night, and then she would recover.

But Indians were often less able to resist such nameless ills. Angus Haws had known whole tribes to be wiped out by something that gave a white man the sniffles. He had never thought to wonder why.

She was an Arapaho, patient and gentle and quiet. She had been with him two years. Her name, Wo-Man, a simple name of her own choosing, was the result of a misunderstanding.

Two years before, in the spring of 1845, Haws had been retrieving one of his traps from deep grass on the shore of a lake in mountains farther north. The beaver that had triggered the trap during the night had, instead of diving instinctively into deeper water, struggled to the bank, dragging the five-pound trap that had crushed one hind leg. A full-grown male with a fine winter pelt, he had tried to chew off the lower portion of the leg, but in his thrashings he had become entangled in the grass and brush along the shore until at last he had weakened and died. Kneeling on one knee to release the jaws of the trap, Haws had sensed movement behind him. There had been no sound louder than the crushing of grass under a moccasined foot, but Haws had whirled and ducked as a tomahawk slashed toward his head.

Missing flesh and bone, the honed edge of stone tore a long rent in his buckskin jacket. That pull combined with his hasty movement to spill Haws onto his back. In falling, his leg came up to meet the Indian's unexpected attack. His foot smashed into the man's naked belly and lifted him high. The momentum of his charge carried him over Haws's head and into the water.

As the Indian came up spluttering, still holding his tomahawk in his hand, Angus Haws was diving toward him, one hand sliding his skinning knife from the sheath attached to his belt. The impact of his huge body bowled the Indian over. Together they went under water. Haws's left hand caught the Indian's wrist to prevent another blow with the tomahawk, which was ineffective under water. His right hand drove a tongue of steel in an upward thrust into the Indian's belly—up to Green River.

When he withdrew his blade the redskin fell away. He surfaced once and then disappeared. Haws turned away, already wiping his knife on his blackened shirt sleeve.

He found the woman hiding in the forest near his camp along with two ponies and her warrior's gear packed onto a travois. The Indian, a loner traveling with his woman and baby, had plundered Haws's camp in his absence, stealing pelts and robes and cooking utensils. Not satisfied, he had thought to steal the mountain man's traps as well.

Later Angus Haws traded the Indian ponies. He kept the woman.

She had proved docile and submissive from the beginning, either from fear for her baby or simple awe of Haws himself, whose sudden appearance before her, huge and hairy and wet, was frightening enough.

His first words to her, after dragging her in silence back to his camp, were, "Ye're his woman?"

"Wo-Man?"

"That's it." A finger jabbed at her chest. "His woman?" Haws's glance went toward the lake. "He's fishbait now."

Her black-cherry eyes studied him, unreadable. She hugged her child tighter to her breast. At last she nodded. "Wo-Man," she said. It was acquiescence in the inevitable. It was also a name.

The child, a weakling girl, had died that following autumn. The woman had lived with Haws for all of two years, serving him in the fashion of her people. She provided the comfort of a tipi, erecting it after Haws had felled trees for the long poles, fashioning the hide cover and keeping it in good repair. She did all of the cooking. She treated and sewed leather garments and moccasins for him. She relieved him of the task of fleshing, stretching, and drying the beaver pelts he took in his trapping. And she provided release for the strong lusts of a solitary man.

Now she was dying. Her face, turned toward him above the edge of the buffalo robe under which she lay, was impassive. Her slanted black eyes seemed to have sunk deeper into the round face.

Angus Haws stepped through the entrance hole of the tipi into the open. He stood outside for a moment, feeling the bite of the early morning air in the high mountains, disgruntled, angry without admitting that he felt any grief over the woman. He liked her well enough. She was no trouble, she wasn't lazy, she never complained. He felt nothing as strong as love. Haws simply didn't think of her that way, any more than he had loved any of the Indian wives he had taken at various times over the years, or the women of Ranchos de Taos or of the fort settlements he went to in the late spring of the year with his packs of pelts and his winter hungers.

The only woman for whom Angus Haws had felt the tenderness of love had died when he was twelve years old, in Pennsylvania. He had lived another year in the commune with his father and a dozen brothers and sisters. Love had died with his mother, who had cornsilk hair and a sweet voice when she sang to her children, softly, for singing was frowned upon by the elders of the commune. In that same year Haws

11

was apprenticed to the owner of an ironworks, a member of the commune. He bided his chance and a year later, at the age of thirteen, he ran away.

Some years later he had turned up in St. Louis. As a strapping eighteen-year-old he was hired on by Jedediah Smith, Bill Sublette, and David Jackson for one of the trapping expeditions they mounted after buying out General William Ashley. Haws had learned the trade with the three partners and, later, with the Rocky Mountain Fur Company. In the same year that Smith was killed by Indians on the Santa Fe Trail, in 1831, Haws quit the company to go out on his own. Since then he had been a free trapper most of the time, liking it better that way, taking orders from no one.

Once Haws had traveled to California with Uncle Dick Wootton's party, traveling from Bent's Fort into the Sacramento Valley. Many of the trappers who had gone with him had stayed there, liking the warm climate and the gentler ways of that territory. Haws, restless, had returned to Santa Fe that same winter.

In the years since he had become more and more of a loner, trapping by himself, retreating from the great northern basins like that mighty watershed of the Green River, heavily worked by the big fur companies, into remoter mountain regions, seeking out secret valleys threaded by slow streams and lost lakes. For the last three years he had been trapping in the northern reaches of the territory disputed by the Mexican and American governments. At times he'd had trouble with the Mexican authorities, who had decreed that trapping for outsiders was illegal. Haws had simply stopped going into Taos then, heading instead for Bent's Fort with his load of pelts in the spring.

In the late fall of 1846, the time of the Yellow Leaves, Haws and Wo-Man had come to the isolated string of lakes and streams where he now stood. Wo-Man had raised the tipi and they had settled in. Through the winter he had seen no one, prowling mountain man or renegade Indian. While Wo-Man busied herself around the tipi, cooking and cleaning and treating pelts, Haws went each day across a ridge into a neighboring valley where he worked the beaver waters, alone with the animals and the lakes and the looming mountains, living close to the land like any other animal, liking it that way, wanting nothing else. There had been only about two months of heavy snows during which he could not trap.

Others like himself still wandered and trapped in the high ranges of the Rockies, but they were few, individuals or small parties. Haws seldom even saw other mountain men now, except when he came down into the towns and forts or the camps of friendly Indians. Some were dead.

13

Some had moved on, to Oregon or California, to river-bottom farms or to jobs as scouts and guides for emigrant trains or for military parties like General Stephen Watts Kearny's Army of the West, which had crossed the plains in the late summer past when Haws was at Bent's Fort.

Haws did not miss old friends. Even in the early days with the large trapping parties he had been a solitary man, keeping to himself, chafing under company rules. Angus Haws had never liked taking orders or adapting to other men's needs or whims, or depending on another to watch his back, not since he ran away from the commune and his nest of brothers and sisters, now long forgotten.

Nevertheless he couldn't understand why others of his breed had drifted off to other pursuits. Admittedly the prices paid for beaver pelts had dropped drastically, but that was only temporary. There would always be a demand for the furs. Such things didn't change. It was only a matter of time before the beaver came back. Maybe the price would be up again this year. He would have nearly three hundred pounds of "hairy bank notes" when he reached Bent's Fort. Last year he had sold for an average of only $1.50 a plew, and the fact still rankled. It wasn't long ago that he had gotten five times as much, in the times of the great spring rendezvous, the gatherings along the Green River and the Wind and the Popo Agie.

It struck Haws suddenly that a great deal had changed, almost without his noticing. How many years had it been since the last rendezvous on the Green at Horse Creek, near Fort Bonneville? Five? Six?

It was two winters past that the Arapaho brave tried to tomahawk him. A year before that was the summer of the big floods, in '44. Then there was the year he was jumped by that bunch of Kiowas over on Utah Creek, where he nearly lost his hair. And before that he'd spent a month in jail at Sante Fe and had most of his pelts confiscated, a wasted year. And still another year was the time that grizzly clawed him, and he lived half the winter on bear meat and then sold his skins at Fort Lupton on the South Platte. How many years was that? "Dog me if it ain't bin seven y'ars," Haws muttered. It didn't seem possible. It seemed like only a spring or two back until you stopped to count . . .

The outline of the trees on the ridge east of the tipi was visible now against the first gray light before dawn. It was time to collect his traps.

Haws stepped back inside the tipi, feeling its warmth close around him. Wo-Man's sunken dark eyes watched as he found his wolfskin cap and his rifle. In the dim light from the fire her eyes revealed neither pain nor hope nor grief. They remained patient, asking nothing.

On an impulse he did not examine Haws added

15

a few small branches to the pyramid in the fire pit. Flames licked at them. There was nothing else he could do for her.

And his traps would not wait.

TWO

Angus Haws had had the tipi raised in a clearing behind a ridge that placed a barrier of distance and trees and land between it and the beaver waters he worked. Anyone discovering one would not necessarily or immediately find the other. Twice each day—in the last light of evening to set his traps, again in the first gray of dawn to collect them—he climbed the steep slope to the top of the ridge and made his way down the forested slope on the far side. He moved at ease through the dark shadows that still hugged the ground under the trees, his stride long, his step silent. At any distance, in his buckskin garments he ceased to be a man, if he was visible at all. He might have been a deer or some other animal of the mountains and the woods. But more dangerous.

He was a tall man, three inches over six feet, with broad, heavy shoulders, barrel chest, and arms like small tree trunks. His belly was flat, his hips and buttocks wide. Long, powerful thighs were tightly encased in leggings of soft deerskin, patiently softened by Wo-Man. His long jacket, fringed along the shoulder and arm seams, came to his knees. It was dark with the stains of sweat, animal fat, blood, and smoke. He wore thick, double-soled moccasins of tough buffalo hide, soundless on the needle-covered floor of the forest or in the dew-wet grass.

His hair under the round wolfskin cap was a dark brown, falling to his shoulders, snarled and matted. His beard, of the same coloring but shaded into two or three different hues from chocolate to rusty red, was long and full and tangled. What facial skin showed, stretched over forehead and high cheekbones and the heavy bridge of his nose, was sun-darkened to the shade of old leather, out of which peered two narrow slits of bright blue.

Into the leather belt around his waist had been thrust a flintlock pistol with a 9-inch barrel, .52-caliber to match that of his Hawken rifle, enabling him to use the same bullet mold for each. The rifle, from the works of Jacob and Samuel Hawken of St. Louis, was a flintlock Plains rifle with a heavy, 36-inch octagonal barrel. Haws had been outfitted with it nearly twenty years before when he was with the Smith, Sublette, Jackson group and the Hawken factory supplied rifles for the company. He trusted it over the percussion locks made by the Hawken brothers and others for their newer pieces. In addition to these weapons Haws carried, attached to his belt, his sheathed Green River skinning knife, a small Yankee hatchet, whetstone, awl holder, and scent container. Hanging from a shoulder loop were bullet pouch and powder horn.

Quick, powerful, keen of sense and bristling with weapons, he was a creature to make any other lift its head, sniff and move away. Only the mighty grizzly habitually stood his ground before one of Haws's mountain breed.

A mile east of the forested ridge he reached the bank of a quiet stream, one of a network threading through a grassy meadow toward a finger lake at the north end of the valley. Haws followed the stream until he came to a thick growth of riverbank willows where he had hidden his dugout canoe. It was about eight feet long, hollowed by hand out of a cottonwood log.

Haws pushed away from the bank and drifted silently downstream in the dugout. The surface of the creek was smooth, silvery gray in the early light that frosted the tops of the willows and cottonwoods along the banks and the evergreens on the higher slopes flanking the valley. He was alert, hearing every rustle of movement in the tall grasses on either side, his narrowed gaze studying the ground shadows ahead of him as well as searching for the sets he had made the previous evening.

These were prime beaver waters, the banks of the streams and the narrow lake lined with tempting willow and cottonwood sprouts, tender greens and young trees. Haws had read the presence of beaver the previous day from trees felled to get at the bark of the high branches, and from other signs the beaver left to mark his trail—mounds of mud and twigs impregnated with castoreum, the same glandular secretions Haws used to bait his traps, and the evidence of gnawed sticks and discarded knots, the garbage set adrift in the current.

At his first trap Haws nudged his log canoe into the bank. He stripped down to a flannel breechclout and, almost naked, eased into the icy water. His leathers, had he worn them, would have dried as hard as boards. He had set his traps after a water approach in his canoe, leaving as little human scent as possible. The trap was placed a few inches under water at the edge of the stream, a tender willow shoot placed above it in the open, just above water, the end dipped in castoreum.

He had caught a mature young male. The beaver, approaching the baited willow stick, had stepped onto the pan of the trap as he lifted his nose to the bait. In panic he had dived for deeper water, dragging the trap with him. The trap was chained to a stake farther out, and the stake had held. The beaver had drowned in the deep water near the center of the stream.

Haws returned to the dugout with the carcass.

Working quickly, he made a long cut down the belly of the dead animal, and crosscuts along the insides of the legs. He chopped off all four feet. Then he stripped the pelt from the carcass and used his knife to scrape away adhering bits of flesh and fat. He retained the tail, not for its fur but for its sweet, succulent meat, a welcome treat after a long diet of venison. The rest of the beaver was edible enough, even good to eat, but he had no need of it, with deer and elk cuts packed in a skin bag on the shady side of the tipi. Haws tossed the carcass into the brush away from the shoreline.

His second trap had been set in the same quiet feeder stream near the mouth of the lake. Before he reached it he spotted the float stick riding the quiet current. Like the other trapped beaver, this one had plunged for the middle of the stream. His thrashings had uprooted the stake Haws had driven into the muddy bottom, but the animal had drowned all the same, held under by the weight of the trap and the six-foot length of chain. The floating stake led Haws directly to his catch.

He had placed his remaining four traps along the eastern shore of the finger lake. Here his luck had not been as good. One trap was untouched— approaching beaver had been either disturbed or suspicious, warned by Haws's scent conflicting with the tempting beaver smell. In two other traps the jaws had closed on a foot or leg but the animal had managed to struggle onto the bank or a shallow shelf. One beaver had gnawed off a foot and escaped. The other, a youngster by the size of the severed limb, had lost most of a leg. Crippled, the two survived to become easier prey for other hunters. Only in the last of his six traps did Haws find his third catch.

The sun was high now, the day warming as Haws's knife flashed in the sunlight, alternately shining steel or red. He worked without thought, his mind a blank, but in these hours of the morning he was totally alive, a creature as completely free as those he trapped or hunted, aware of the sun's warmth and the vaulting sky, nostrils quivering to the smells of fresh spring grasses and wildflowers, earth and water and animal blood, feeling the massive weight of the high mountains shouldering against the blue above him, knowing all this without thought because he was part of it, one with it, hunter and hunted, part of nature's endless cycle.

His work done, he paddled slowly across the narrow end of the lake and back up the slow stream. He cached his dugout in the same willow thicket where he had hidden it the night before. He had left his undisturbed trap in place. The other five he carried with him, along with his three fresh pelts and the broad flat tails he had saved for their sweet meat.

He returned the way he had come up the long

slope to the crest of the timbered ridge that overlooked his tipi. The thin smoke from the fire had not been visible beyond the ridge. Now, as he came within sight of the cone-shaped lodge, partially screened by a grove of pine and aspen, he saw that there was no smoke at all. The fire had gone out.

Angus Haws sensed danger.

As yet he had seen nothing. There was no clear sign to explain the feeling of danger. He knew it as an animal does, in the tingling of nerve ends, the tightening of his belly, the quivering of his nostrils.

Cautiously he moved down the steep, wooded western flank of the ridge. Halfway down he hid his traps and his morning's take of pelts and tails under wild berry brush. He covered the last part of the slope in a crouch, moving from tree to tree as quickly as a bird darts from one branch to another, visible only as a patch of hair and a slit of blue peering past the trunk of a pine, his darkened leathers hardly distinguishable from the tree's bark.

He brought his powder horn around to the front, in handy position, and popped two lead balls into his mouth. A third was already in place with its charge of powder, secured by a tallow-greased patch firmly seated by the thrust of the hickory rod.

At the edge of the woods Haws stopped and

waited. He had approached from the north where the cover was thicker and there was the widest stretch of clearing between him and the tipi, a distance of some fifty yards. At that distance he could drive in a nail with his rifle, hammering the nail deeper with successive blows of his lead balls. The Hawken rifle fired in an almost flat trajectory over distances up to 150 yards. Angus Haws could shoot the branch from under a sparrow at 200 yards without harming the bird. With an ordinary powder charge, the slow twist of the Hawken rifling gave almost no recoil. Even with the heavier charge Haws had poured down the barrel—not knowing what he might have to bring down—the kick would hardly be notice-able. It would not affect the deadly accuracy of his shooting at all.

Puzzled, Haws crouched at the edge of the clearing. He smelled nothing, heard nothing. But something was there. A prowling animal? Indians? A trapper like himself, someone who had watched him earlier, who had seen him beyond the ridge and sneaked up to the tipi in safety to steal his pelts?

Lips pursed behind his matted beard, Haws was skeptical. He had seen no Indian sign, and he didn't believe any white man could have lurked nearby for long without his knowing it.

The grass around the tipi, worn down by his own and Wo-Man's activity, provided no clue.

A half-dozen pelts hung outside, stretched on willow hoops to dry, the flesh side turned up to face the sun. These were undisturbed.

Haws dropped back into the woods and circled a dozen yards farther to his right. Creeping close to the edge of the clearing once more, he squinted toward the tipi.

One whole side had been torn open, the tough hide cover ripped like paper. Even as he saw this Haws heard a heavy thumping and growling, as if a man in a drunken rage were trampling and smashing everything he could seize. Understanding came instantly, and Haws thought of Wo-Man, lying helpless inside the lodge in her buffalo robes.

Then the grizzly burst through the gaping hole.

The huge bear was the mountain man's special enemy, and the feeling often seemed mutual. Of all animals of the mountains, these were the two who were accustomed to taking what they wanted whenever they found it.

Angus Haws did not wait for the bear to discover him. He stepped out from behind a pine, raised his flintlock rifle, aimed and squeezed off a shot in a swift, fluid movement, sending a lead ball crashing into the bear's chest.

The grizzly reared up with a roar, standing a full eight feet tall. Then he charged. Heavy and cumbersome, his lumbering gait appearing slow to the eye, he covered the distance between the tipi and the edge of the woods where Haws stood his ground with startling swiftness. The mountain man poured powder down the rifle barrel and followed it with a lead ball. By the time he had the load seated and lifted the crescent-shaped butt of the half-stock to his shoulder, the bear was only twenty yards away. Teeth and gums and red tongue were visible in his snarling mouth. Haws fired point-blank, knowing that he couldn't miss, knowing that he had placed his first ball in the vicinity of the great bear's heart, but knowing, too, that there was no animal harder to bring down and that one swipe of one of those broad, taloned paws could rip him open end to end.

The grizzly staggered as the half-ounce ball of lead smashed into his chest. Still he came on, the momentum of his charge hardly seeming to be slowed.

Angus Haws dropped back. The bear crashed into the woods behind him, trampling over brush that Haws dodged around. Trying to reach him, the bear blundered blindly into a pine tree. The tree shivered, and the earth itself seemed to quake. "Waugh!" Haws muttered aloud—the familiar mountain man's cry that was part grunt, part exclamation, part war cry, suitable for all occasions.

There was no opportunity to load and fire the Hawken rifle again. The grizzly was too close.

Only the dense growth of junipers kept him from reaching Haws in his rage.

Haws dragged his flintlock pistol from under his belt, already loaded. He fired across his body. The grizzly gave another loud bellow. A paw swung. It ripped bark and a chunk of wood from the trunk of a pine at the level of a man's head.

The bear stopped then, head lowered and swaying. A gush of bright red spurted from his open mouth. He leaned against a tree as if he were tired. Then he toppled over.

For a moment Haws stood in the pine grove, breathing hard. Loading his rifle deliberately, he approached the huge bear with caution. It proved needless. The grizzly was dead. He had been dead, Haws knew, when the first bullet struck his chest. A proud animal rage had kept him going. Haws could understand that.

Little given to exclamation, Haws stared down at the fallen bear and muttered aloud, "Ye was some. Ye surely was."

THREE

Hunger and curiosity, Haws guessed, had brought the grizzly to the tipi. He was a curious and fearless creature. The hunger had led him to Haws's cache of meat. It might have been curiosity that caused him to swipe a paw at Wo-Man lying in her buffalo robe. It was argued by some that a sleeping human was safe from attack by the great bear, but that sage piece of lore had not saved the Indian woman. One side of her face had been laid open.

Haws wondered if she already had been dead when the grizzly invaded the lodge, for she had not tried to crawl away, or if she had watched with those patient black-cherry eyes, too weak to evade the careless swing of curving talons.

Unmoved by what had become too familiar, Angus Haws turned to an inspection of the damage the grizzly had done. He had eaten much of the packed meat, and he had found and ripped open two of Haws's pressed and thong-bound packs of dried beaver plews. Haws could not tell immediately how many of the furs had been destroyed. Cooking utensils and other gear were scattered about, but there was little else that could be harmed.

After a while he carried a shovel to the soft ground near the trees and began to dig a shallow grave. He felt neither pity nor grief. Working under the noon sun, his powerful arms and shoulders lifting and driving methodically, he was soon sweating under his leather shirt. The sweat loosened his muscles and made the digging easier. Mindless in his labors, he kept on until it was done.

FOUR

A week later Angus Haws left the mountains, riding a large gray horse, leading two pack horses. He had rescued nearly one hundred and eighty whole beaver plews from the depredations of the grizzly. One horse carried two full packs of pelts weighing approximately one hundred pounds each. The second pack horse was burdened with the remainder of the good pelts along with Haws's traps, spare parts, cooking utensils, and other gear. Luckily no more than thirty of the beaver skins had been so badly torn that he had had to discard them, those being on top of his tightly pressed packs when the grizzly pawed them. The salvaged plews represented all of his fall and spring trapping.

He left nothing behind but the torn tipi and a rock-covered mound at the edge of the clearing. Reaching the ridge line as he rode away, he did not look back.

ONE

Despair, Ter Bryant thought. Despair began when the first mastodon got bogged down in a quagmire.

There were twelve men on the wagon, slipping and sliding and falling in the quicksand pits of the shallow creek that flowed into the Arkansas. Twelve men and double mule teams ahead, and a bed of boughs and brush laid over the soft spots to give purchase for the digging wheels. All that and the wagon was hardly moving.

Jaine Bryant sat on the board seat of the wagon, pale under the deep shade of her bonnet's hood, no longer holding the reins. They were in the hands of young Jeremy Rhoads, a strong boy of fifteen, who shouted and slapped the long leathers with boyish excitement and enthusiasm, too young to know despair. The men heaved on the wheels and the Mexican drover shouted and cursed at the mules in Spanish as he cracked his whip. The wheels kept turning, ever so slowly, and the wagon inched forward across the wide shallows. It had to be kept moving, however slowly, for the moment it stopped the wheels began to sink.

Now here was Long Tom Brock, the wagon caravan's chief hunter and scout, a tall black man with an on-again, off-again French accent and vocabulary, who claimed indeed to be a Frenchman, shucking off his moccasins and wading barefoot through sand and water to throw his weight against the wheels. And whether it was the strength of another shoulder or simply that the front wheels dug into solid ground at last, the wagon suddenly surged forward. A cheer went up, a few hats flew in the air.

There was a narrow strand of cottonwoods along a section of the west bank of the creek, near where the wagons emerged up the slope that had been cut into the bank. The trees were woven among thickets of plum berries and wild roses, grapes and cherries and young willows, the only green freshness anywhere in sight in this area of rolling brown prairie. Ter Bryant saw the white of his young wife's face and had the wagon driven over to this shade.

"You can step down and rest here," he called up to Jaine, smiling through the dust and mud that caked his face, not letting any of his anxious concern show. She'd had a hard time these past few days with dysentery, blamed on the alkaline water, and he didn't like the way she had thinned out so suddenly, or the dark hollows out of which her soft gray eyes watched him, huge in the unnatural boniness of her face. "Plenty of time to stretch your legs. It'll be high noon before the wagons are all across. Chances are we won't move out until the sun's gone down a little."

She nodded, her smile wan. He helped her down from the high wagon seat and saw her to a patch of shade.

"You'll be all right now?"

"I'm fine, Ter. Don't worry about me."

He had to leave her, for one of the big wagons was starting down the far bank amidst a flurry of shouts and urgings. But he could not leave all worry behind.

For a while he forgot, down in the sandy bottom of the creek, sweating streams of his own to run down and merge with the shallow current, hauling and pushing and shouting under a sky like a shiny skillet in the unrelenting heat that climbed over 100° at midday. But every once in a while he would look up when he came to the west bank where she rested under the cottonwoods, and he would catch a glimpse of her blue dress and of her hair. She had removed her bonnet in the shade, revealing hair a dark burnished color like old brass, done up in pigtails for traveling and folded neatly across her head like a coronet. The sight of her touched him as it always did, but now it brought a pang of worry.

These had been trying weeks, and the worst,

Long Tom Brock promised solemnly, lay ahead, in the hostile and Indian lands they must cross and in the high passes of the mountains beyond. Five weeks since the train pulled away from Westport Landing, shepherded by a full company of dragoons from Leavenworth. More weeks of traveling and waiting before that, going back to the day they rode out of Natchez on the steamer, looking back and waving while the figures on the wharf grew smaller and smaller, lost at last in the bustle of the waterfront, Jaine's parents and her brother Jonathan, Ter's own brothers and sisters and his mother, all smiling and waving and trying to look happy, Ter's two brothers unable to hide their envy.

Sometimes Bryant still found it hard to believe that it had all happened. He had met Jaine MacDonald on an excursion boat returning to Natchez from New Orleans. He'd taken one look into the depths of those gray eyes and he was lost, he knew he had to have her. It didn't matter that she was the only daughter of a thrifty and thriving planter on the Hill, a long way above the Bryants. One day soon James MacDonald would have prospered enough to command one of those great mansions on the bluffs overlooking the Mississippi. Ter Bryant, by contrast, had grown up in the rough-and-ready battleground of lower Natchez, a haven of thieves and drunkards and gamblers (like his father) and boisterous rivermen. True, he'd climbed up the Hill far enough to take a job as a bank cashier, surely respectable enough, but he would not forget the first time he came calling on Jaine MacDonald at her father's house, nor the look of skepticism in MacDonald's eyes. And the time came, after he had discovered the wonder of Jaine returning his love, when Ter Bryant knew that he could not live forever in the same town with his father-in-law, under his considerable shadow.

They had married in the fall, James MacDonald reluctantly giving his consent when he saw that his daughter's heart and mind were set unyieldingly. All through the winter there had been news of great happenings in the Far West. Every event fired Ter Bryant's imagination with new longings. At the time of his wedding Zachary Taylor had been defeating the Mexicans at Monterrey, and General Stephen Watts Kearny, having occupied Santa Fe without firing a shot, had marched onward to California, where Kearny and Commodore Robert Stockton had both figured in the routing of the Mexicans at San Gabriel in January. Rebellion put down in Taos in February! General Winfield Scott landing at Veracruz in March! All of northern Mexico coming under the American flag! Each headline made him more restless.

They said Ter Bryant was a dreamer, like his father, who had met a violent end in a tavern brawl when Ter was a boy. That winter he dreamed great dreams. Through the long nights he talked endlessly to Jaine about the new lands that were now opening up, the dynasties that would be founded in New Mexico and California, the fortunes that would be made by those with the courage and foresight to stake their claims. He spoke of the great mountains and mighty rivers and countless buffalo herds of the western plains, of danger and bravery and glory (but not so much of danger). He didn't talk of the severe limits on his future in Natchez, where a respectable job in a cashier's cage was all that he could look forward to. Whether he wore Jaine down or converted her with his own enthusiasm, or whether she simply saw his need and, in her quiet way, accepted it, Ter Bryant didn't know. In the end he won out. He left his job, and in early April they traveled upriver to Missouri. There, with all he had in the world, Ter outfitted their wagon and began the overland journey to Westport Landing, where the wagon caravan was to set out under the fortunate protection of the dragoons.

Ter Bryant had never before traveled west of the Mississippi. He had had no way of anticipating what lay in store for him and his nineteen-year-old bride. Bryant had not had a coddled youth. He'd learned to fight on the waterfront with fists and boots. He could use a knife, and he was an excellent shot with a rifle. At twenty-four he could work a sixteen-hour day in heat or cold and be up again the next morning, stiff and sore but ready to go. He had camped out and hunted since his early teens, relishing that life far more than his days in the bank. The exhausting journey was not so hard on him.

But he hadn't known how it would be. Imagination couldn't conjure up the agonizing struggles to cross creeks swollen by spring rains, nor the endless clouds of dust that the iron-clad wagon wheels churned up across the arid stretches of the great prairie. No painter had ever accurately portrayed the real emptiness of this immense land, the mind-assaulting distances, the rolling seas of grasses stretching on beyond sight, the blasts of hot air that cracked lips and left eyes burning, the jarring monotony of the slow wagon crawl, like a string of flies inching across an enormous ceiling, nor the sudden cracking violence of the thunder and lightning storms that boiled unchecked across the empty plain. The dust and rain, mosquitoes and flies, rivers and canyons and strange waters, all had taken their toll of Jaine far more than of him. Ter Bryant had seemed to thrive on it all, as if this was what he was meant for. At night, tasting the cool evening air, feeling all around him the sense of limitless space and freedom, he had felt an exhilaration that made him forget aching muscles and parched lips and all the daily exasperations. Jaine had ridden uncomplaining in the wagon, handling the reins much of the time, but he had seen the strain in her face and in her darkening eyes, the flicker of unease when campfire talk turned, as it often did, to the menace of Indians along the trail.

Now, for almost a week, she had been wracked by illness, as many others in the train were, men and women.

Had he been wrong to force this on her? Ter Bryant hated even to ask the question, but it kept recurring each time he glimpsed her sitting alone in the shade on the far bank of the creek, listless and pale where she had always been so lively and spirited at home, in her own environment, in the gentle life she knew on the Hill in her father's house.

He'd make it up to her. Since the first moment he had looked into her gray eyes he had known that he would do anything for her, anything to win her smile and to earn her love. Now it was she who had given up everything for him without complaint—family, friends, a life of ease, all the familiar things and people and places she knew. He'd make it up to her a hundredfold!

"She be fine, lad," someone said.

Ter Bryant turned, startled. Tom Brock was regarding him thoughtfully as the two stood panting on the riverbank, watching the unwieldy bulk of a freight wagon lumber safely up the inclined bank. The pace of the mule teams quickened as they felt the wagon pull free of the dragging bottom.

"It's de water," Brock said. "She be over it soon. By gar, she be tougher than you think. This child knows."

Brock nodded wisely. Beneath the sometime accent and the occasional French, there was a pleasant cadence in the black man's speech suggestive of the Caribbean islands. Bryant wondered where he had come from and what his life had been, for the endless prairie and the far mountains were familiar ground to him. Huge in his darkened buckskins, his face and hands as black as pitch, he was a striking figure. He had a deep, rumbling laugh and an easy friendliness that had caused Bryant to like him from their first meeting. He wondered how the scout had known what he was thinking. Had his frequent anxious glances been so transparent?

"I hope you're right," Bryant said.

"She be a mighty fine woman," Long Tom said, and something glowed in his dark eyes. "You be a lucky man, and you so green." He grinned, white teeth flashing. "Time you gits to California, she be leadin' you a dance, lad. Ain't sure you's man enough to keep up."

"All the man she needs," Bryant retorted.

But he grinned back at the big man in buckskins,

reassured more than the brief exchange warranted on the face of it, taking heart.

Ahead were the mountains, and beyond them, California. It would all be different there.

TWO

In the afternoon the train passed the Lower Crossing of the Arkansas. South of the river, winding through sand hills and disappearing into the parched plain beyond, was the shorter trail to Santa Fe, already cut deep into the land, as plain as a road. This trace in the years to come would become known as the Cimarron Cutoff. Many of the traders and emigrants looked wistfully across the river, thinking of the days of plodding travel that could have been saved if the caravan had crossed here. All were weary of the trail now, weary of dust and heat and monotony, weary of one another's company, longing for the sight of unfamiliar faces, of civilized buildings and real beds and meals other than wild game.

But the rumors of Indian troubles all across the Southern Plains persisted, confirmed by every traveler. Seeing the white men and the Mexicans at war among themselves, the more aggressive tribes had become bolder, striking with increasing liberty at hunting parties and caravans. Comanches, Kiowas, Utes, Pawnees, all were on the warpath—something Ter had not counted on in his winter plans for their journey, Jaine Bryant thought, glancing at the man who rode beside her in the wagon. He had made light of the Indian danger, eyes snapping with excitement rather than fear at the prospect. But he wouldn't deliberately have led her into danger. He was as worried now as any of them.

With that danger real, no one in the caravan was prepared to strike off along the shorter trail without the military escort, and Lieutenant Cole's dragoons were under orders to continue along the Arkansas to Bent's Fort. The wagons would go with them, even though it meant a longer journey.

Of the sixteen wagons in the caravan, not counting the military, six belonged to traders, the rest to emigrants. Of the latter there were nineteen men, six women, and eleven children. Jaine Bryant was the only woman childless with the train. She was quite different from the others in other ways, too, ten years younger on the average, seeming frail and green and ill-suited to such an arduous enterprise.

But she wasn't fragile, Jaine thought with stubborn pride. She wasn't useless or unable to endure hardship. She had stood up to the daily pounding of the wagon wheels under her as well as any, except for this past week when the dysentery had struck her. She was ashamed of her sickness, but she hadn't been alone in being affected by the water and heat. At least two men were still sick in their wagons, unable to sit up. She was once more riding beside her husband, taking the reins at times, able to cook meals and do her share.

She hated being sick, and she hated the weakness that she felt now from the wrenching attacks. But she was pulling out of it.

She wondered how much of Ter's worry was over her. She didn't want that. She had undertaken to follow him wherever he went, as long as they lived. She didn't want to be a burden to him, or to make him doubt his decision on this first leg of their long journey together.

Jouncing along, she studied her husband with sidelong glances. Black Irish, he called himself, his hair being very thick and black and curly. He wore mustaches, grown luxuriant on the trail, drooping down on either side of his mouth. His eyes were a lively blue, striking with his black hair. His face was now deeply burned by wind and sun. He was of more than average height, crowding six feet, built more along the lines of a racehorse than one meant for the plow. But the body she had come to know so intimately was lean and hard. During these recent weeks she had been aware of changes in it, the toughening of his muscles, the burning away of every excess ounce, the new ease with which he could lift her toward her seat or sweep her down from the height of a wagon wheel. He was the equal of any man in the caravan in handling a horse or a team of mules, or in meeting a sudden crisis. More than equal, she thought.

Taking this gamble had been right for him. He was growing before her eyes, finding himself, reaching within to discover and test the best in himself.

Had she ever doubted him? No, never. She would have been happy with her bank cashier in Natchez, but lately she had begun to realize that, with Ter, she too was reaching out for a life that would be larger, more vivid, more challenging and, in the end, surely more rewarding. Not easy, not safe, not secure and predictable, none of these things that her father had wanted for her. Strange that her mother had understood better than her father why Ter Bryant was the right man for her. Or perhaps it was not strange at all.

Ahead of the wagon a series of mounds appeared off to the right, obscured by the haze of heat and dust. Prairie dogs popped up to look and vanished into their holes. And among them, as Jaine had learned, breeding caution, rattlesnakes curled in the shade.

Almost lost in the dust that rose from the caravan were the blue-clad soldiers from Leavenworth. Peering in their direction, Jaine saw a pool slowly dissolve into nothingness. Another mirage, she thought in wonder, so clear and real that she had seemed to see the sky mirrored on its surface, a hawk slowly wheeling against the blue.

Far off on the horizon she thought she could see a stand of trees, and beyond them a line of blue hills. Were they real or another trick of this bewildering prairie? How she could long, if she permitted herself to, for the dark shelter of one of the great oaks that stood around her family's house in Natchez, where she had swung as a child from a swing attached to a sturdy branch. She had known heat there, but nothing like this dry, withering oven that sucked the juices from her body and left her parched and gasping. And at home there was always shade. Here there was none for miles on end.

When would she see a mountain clad in green?

Jaine Bryant glanced again at her husband. She drew herself up, half guiltily, and touched dry lips with the tip of her tongue. Home was not the place they had left behind, she told herself with the vehemence of doubt. Home was the place they would find.

THREE

That night came their first brush with Indians.

The wagons had kept on the move until well after dark, at last forming a corral at Bear Creek, across the way from its junction with the

Arkansas. The circle was tightly enclosed, the forward wheel of one wagon nesting against a hind wheel of the one ahead. All the loose livestock and the mules were turned inside the corral, except for the horses of the dragoons, which were picketed separately just beyond the circle of wagons where the soldiers themselves made camp.

The Bryants had bedded down along with most of the weary travelers. Only the sentries and a few men more used to this wilderness were up and about. Long Tom Brock, who had been sharing the Bryants' cooking fire, still sat there, silently smoking his pipe, slapping occasionally at a mosquito, listening to the hoot of an owl or the distant yowling of a coyote. He was waiting for his midnight turn at sentinel duty.

From the west end of the corral came a sudden commotion. Shouts rose, a flurry of hoofbeats drummed, a rifle cracked. Brock rose quickly, his long rifle already in hand. The noise woke Ter Bryant. In his haste to rise he became tangled in his blankets. By the time he was on his feet the cry was sweeping along the line of wagons like dry leaves caught in a gust of wind: "Indians!"

Then Lieutenant Cole was galloping around the outer curve of the wagon circle, shouting, "Fort up! Indians!"

While Ter Bryant bundled Jaine over behind one of the big wheels of their wagon, Tom

Brock kicked dirt over the fire, extinguishing it instantly. There were shouts and cries all around them now, then another rattle of gunfire, like fireworks crackling.

Then silence.

Almost as suddenly as the alarm had come it was all over. Among the emigrants questions were called out, answers given, rumors exaggerated. A score of dragoons shortly rode by, close to the Bryant wagon, harness clinking and squeaking, the men silent. They disappeared into the darkness.

Finally a trooper made the rounds with news. Indians had attacked, but they had been after horses, not scalps. One sentry was dead, another wounded. It was suspected that the dead man might have been asleep, although the trooper bearing the news denied it. There had been no outcry. The first alarm was given by the second sentry as he warded off the attack of a half-naked savage, who had escaped unhurt. Twenty horses, one entire picket line, had been lost by the dragoons. Only the timely warning of the surviving sentry had saved the remaining horses. Dragoons were in pursuit of the thieves.

An hour later Lieutenant Cole himself made his way among the wagons, calming excited civilians, seemingly undisturbed by the loss of the horses or the knowledge that marauding red-skins were in the vicinity. Or he was putting up a fine front, Ter Bryant thought, his own excitement hardly calmed at all by an hour's waiting and speculation.

The Indians had got away with the stolen horses, disappearing either across the river or into the hollows of the rolling prairie. It had been deemed unwise to send a large party after them, the dragoons being needed to protect the wagons in case the theft of the horses was prelude to a direct attack on the caravan. But the immediate threat was over; everyone could return to his blankets.

But for the rest of that night, in spite of fatigue, there was little sleep. The buzz of talk around the wagons lasted until first light streaked the eastern horizon. As it climbed and day bloomed over the land, as if a giant wick had been turned up, it revealed the empty bluffs on the far bank of the river, the thick turf of short grasses lately dotting this part of the plains, the lonely sweep of the prairie, empty as far as the eye could see.

ONE

Bent's Fort!

Through the heat waves the huge, impregnable mud fortress rose out of the harsh, treeless prairie like a mirage at first. Then it took on solidity. Incredible as it was, it was real, a testament to the vision and enterprise of Charles Bent and his brother William, who had set their mud castle in the heart of hostile Indian territory and used it to build a wilderness empire.

What a parade of men had passed through here—Kit Carson and Peg-Leg Smith, Old Bill Williams, Jim Beckwourth and Joe Walker, the Bents' partner, Ceran St. Vrain, General Stephen Watts Kearny, and John Charles Frémont and a host of others, all the pioneering adventurers whose exploits had fueled Ter Bryant's dreams.

Excitement ripped through the caravan like a flash flood. Lieutenant Cole and a detachment of his dragoons rode on ahead to meet the welcoming party from the fort, and many of the men from the wagons jumped on horses and raced forward, leaving the wagons to crawl over the last miles in their dust. Ter Bryant, feeling the excitement as this first great goal of the overland journey was in sight, could hardly contain himself. But he stayed with Jaine and the wagon, holding the reins, grinning as the Mexican mule skinners, who were themselves delighted to be so close to their beloved mountains, cursed and whipped the teams.

Out of the haze the lodges of Indians began to appear. The hides with which the tipis were covered were so much the color of the prairie that for a long time they were almost invisible. Suddenly there were countless tipis in sight, a score or more ranging along the east wall outside the fort, others on the low sand hills south of the river where a whole village was encamped. Bryant saw more than a hundred Indians lining the far bank to watch the approach of the horse soldiers and the wagons behind them. Wiry Indian ponies were tethered at one end of the village. Numberless dogs ran around barking. Smoke rose in thin plumes from cooking fires. Copper-skinned figures, young and old, moved among the lodges—more Indians than he had ever thought to see in one place.

Bryant glanced at Jaine. Instead of fear he saw a reflection of his own keen interest. Clearly these were not hostiles but friendly Indians, gathered near the fort to trade—"buffalo robes for baubles and whiskey," Long Tom Brock had said. Mostly they would be Cheyennes and Arapahoes, who alone among the Southern Plains tribes had not joined in this summer's raids against white caravans.

Across from the Cheyenne village, chalk cliffs and shoulders of rock thrust upward from the bottomland. Set back almost a hundred yards from these bare bluffs, on a bench that commanded a view of the prairie for miles around, was the massive adobe castle of the plains.

The wagons swung north—Bryant saw Tom Brock riding in the van beside a buckskin-clad and bearded man from the fort—and drew up near the main entrance to the fort, which faced north away from the river. There was much confusion and noise and conflicting shouts before order slowly came to the scene. The fort was crowded, and after some consultation it was determined that there wasn't room inside for all the soldiers and the emigrant wagons. The wagons were formed into a corral north of the entrance. A detail of dragoons and volunteers was set out to stand watch. The wagons also came under the protection of the cannon mounted in the cylindrical northeast tower.

From somewhere Long Tom Brock appeared, grinning hugely. He beckoned Ter Bryant and Jaine to follow him through the heavy, iron-sheathed gates, set into walls nearly three feet thick and high enough so that three men standing

49

on one another's shoulders would barely be able to reach the top. A watchtower and belfry rose directly over the entry gates.

The huge *placita* was crowded with animals and people. Bryant saw all kinds of strange faces and stranger garb—Mexicans, Indians, mountain men, travelers dressed in Eastern finery, soldiers in uniform. There were rooms built along both sides of the long courtyard, rising two stories high along the west wall, fronted by roofed verandas and balconies supported by sturdy beams. Following Tom Brock, his mind trying to sort out the confusion of color and noise, Ter Bryant felt Jaine's hand clinging tightly to his arm, and it was only then that he began to realize that they were a center of attraction.

No, not both of them. Everyone was staring at Jaine. Grizzled trappers and hunters gaped from their hairy, matted faces. Indians and brown-faced Mexicans pointed and stared and followed her. Suddenly Bryant realized that the grace and beauty he took for granted was causing all the excitement. Few white women of any kind had made the journey across the plains to the fort, and only one, Susan Magoffin, as Bryant would learn later, passing through the previous summer with her husband and General Kearny on the way to Santa Fe, had caused such a stir. Jaine was young, slender, lovely as a picture, her face now flushed from nervous excitement. She had worn a simple muslin dress that morning, knowing that they would reach the fort, and a plain straw bonnet trimmed with blue ribbon, but the outfit looked neither simple nor plain on her. She might have been a lady stepping from her carriage in Natchez or New Orleans. The full skirt that emphasized her narrow waist, the shaped bodice that did not conceal the rounding contours of her bosom, the dark gold hair peeping from under the white bonnet, the light and graceful movements, all these were watched by every man in the fort within sight of her.

As they reached a flight of outside steps leading to an upstairs room along the west wall, Ter Bryant's attention was caught by a great hulking man in dirty buckskins, fringed everywhere so that he seemed to drip strings of leather. He was as tall as Tom Brock, who had nodded briefly as he passed the stranger, but heavier, as broad and thick as a good-sized oak. His matted beard and skin were the color of old bark. What arrested Bryant's gaze was the brightness of the man's blue eyes and the intensity of his stare as Jaine went by him and up the steps. At the top, looking back, Bryant saw the mountain man still staring up at Jaine until she disappeared.

Then the blue eyes caught Bryant's own, which were of the same color but deeper, and locked. For an instant the two men neither moved nor blinked, as if some unspoken challenge flashed between them. Bryant thought he saw a flicker of something like anger in the narrowed eyes. The bite of that look first startled, then puzzled him. Then came an answering, intuitive anger of his own.

But as suddenly as it had come the moment was gone. The tall man in the courtyard below turned away, blending into the flurry of activity accompanying the arrival at the fort of so many wagons and troops.

Bryant found Tom Brock beside him on the deck, looking down at the crowded *placita*. "That tall man, Tom, did you notice him? That one over there in buckskins."

The black man nodded slowly. In his soft accent he said, "He be a mountain man. This child knows him, sure."

"Who is he?"

"He be Angus Haws. Some time, we trap together, long time ago, with de fur company. By gar, he is some, that one."

"You know him well? He was a friend of yours?"

Brock shook his head. "Man like that, he go his own way. Ain't nobody know him, what be inside of him." Brock looked off as if seeing across great distances, finding Haws and himself in some faraway place and time. "*Mon ami*? *Non, non.*" White teeth flashed. "*Vous etre mon ami, eh*? Not that one. He be like de grizzly bear, he don't need no friend. You stay clear of that one, lad. He be trouble."

Ter Bryant frowned, surprised by the soft insistence in Tom Brock's tone. "Is that fair, Tom? What trouble could he be to me?"

"You listen to this child, lad. Angus Haws, he don't belong with civilized folks, he belong to de mountains. You best leave him be."

Bryant laughed. "All right, Tom, I wasn't looking for a partner anyway. Chances are I won't ever see him again."

He turned from the bright, swarming activity of the courtyard into the cool dimness of the room where Jaine waited.

TWO

That night the Bryants—because of Jaine, Ter guessed—were entertained by William Bent himself in the large apartment built above the western wall in the southwest corner of the fort. With them were Lieutenant Cole of the dragoons; Cal Upshaw, captain of the wagon train, and his wife Emily; mountain men Dick Wootton and a French Canadian named Baptiste Cormier; and a traveling journalist from the East called Mansfield.

The apartment left all the guests open-mouthed. It was spacious and well furnished. The dining tables were covered with fine white cloths, and illuminated by buffalo tallow candles. There was a billiard table at one end of the big main room, and a well-stocked bar. Chilled mint juleps were served in fine glasses, William Bent smiling faintly at the astonished reactions of his guests. An icehouse had been built near the river, he confirmed, and the wild mint came from the banks of the Purgatory a dozen miles away.

The host was a slight, intense man, his demeanor clouded by the tragedy that had struck the family that winter when Charles Bent, after having been named the territory's first governor following Kearny's successful occupation of Santa Fe, was slain during the Taos uprising. While William Bent remained withdrawn, talking little, the rest of the conversation was lively and wide-ranging. Much of it had to do with troubles with the Indians. Bent's partner, Ceran St. Vrain, had left the fort early in May with their company's caravan of buffalo robes, beaver pelts and other goods, bound for St. Louis. Word was that the train had been hit by Comanches en route, but had fought off the attack with small losses and continued on to the Mississippi. Mansfield, the journalist, had news of General Winfield Scott's Mexican campaign, driving inland from Veracruz toward Mexico City against spirited opposition. He also carried details of soberer news, confirmed by trappers who had come to the fort from the north during the summer, of the disaster that had struck the Donner party during the winter past, when they were trapped in the high mountains on their way to California. It was said that only a handful of the party had survived after enduring terrible hardship, and there was subdued murmuring among some of the men over other aspects of the tragedy, spoken too low for Jaine Bryant or Emily Upshaw to hear.

The evening's triumph, after all the talk and exchange of news, the chilled mint juleps and a feast of beef and venison and duck, was Jaine's. Even William Bent, dressed in his soft white deerskin shirt and leggings, warmed from his somber mood in her presence, paying court like the other men with innate dignity. Baptiste Cormier played his banjo after supper, and Dick Wootton sang in a raucous but enthusiastic voice. The center of all their attention, Jaine had dressed for the evening in a summer dress of white cotton embroidered with lace and trimmed with pink ribbon. The waist was close-fitting, the sleeves very full. She had fretted over the condition of the dress after weeks in her trunk, but Ter, laughing, had assured her that the men of the fort had probably never seen anyone so lovely.

And so they all said, in their rough words or

with their eyes, and she had her triumph. Even Emily Upshaw joined in smiling tribute, in her own plain middle years happily beyond envy.

Neither Jaine nor Ter Bryant had any way of knowing that this would be the last night she would dress up in her finery for an interminable period, one that would find this happy time receding into memory, becoming unreal, like one of the desert's mirages, as if such joy and pleasure and pride had never been.

After their evening's entertainment the young couple strolled along the rooftop promenade that circled the fort. The roofs of the apartments along the west wall, and the row of storerooms, kitchen, dining hall, and shops along the east wall, were firmly supported and graveled over. A parapet rose about three feet above the roofline, with firing ports set into the wall, so that the graveled roofs became protected defensive positions around the perimeter of the fort in time of attack. But on cool summer evenings like this one, when no danger threatened, the same roofs became a casual promenade.

Below them the huge *placita* was still alive with activity. Troopers sat and smoked after their evening meal. Emigrants gathered in groups or strolled curiously about the fort. Somewhere a fiddle plinked and a few voices rose in song. Ter Bryant could see the fort's well and the giant press used to pack the buffalo hides, and, at the south end of the courtyard, the interior corral and other storage rooms.

They stopped to lean over the parapet, looking out at the shadowed mystery of the prairie, sketched into a wild beauty by the light of a last-quarter moon. Near the river figures sat or stirred about among the tipis in the light of cooking fires. Where fires burned inside the lodges, the upper half of the tipi glowed like a lamp. The lower part of the cover must be a double thickness, Jaine Bryant shrewdly guessed.

The night air was pungent with odors strange and familiar, the rank smell of buffalo hides and beaver pelts from the nearby storage sheds, the smells of bread and simmering meat from the main dining hall, the stench of sweaty, unwashed men and animals, all mingling with the lighter perfumes of smoke and desert flowers and other, nameless scents drifting out of the darkness.

Jaine Bryant felt a sense of wonder that she was here, at this moment, in a world so different from any she had known. Here on the parapet in the darkness the land did not threaten her. She was conscious of a deep, slow quiet beyond the fort's walls, as if one might listen and hear the earth itself slowly turning. The night sky was unimaginably vast over the endless sweep of the prairie. The stars were brighter and clearer and more numerous. In that moment she felt and understood something of the lure of this free, unspoiled land. And yet . . .

"It's some. That's what Tom Brock would say."

"Yes," Jaine agreed. "It's some."

"Are you sorry. Any regrets?"

"That we came?" She smiled at him in the dark. Quieting her misgivings, she said, "No, you were right. It was right for us to find our own way, our own place." It was what you needed, she thought.

"I'm glad you're feeling better. Wasn't that a feast Mr. Bent set out? Did you ever expect to see such a table in this wilderness? And juleps?" He chuckled at the memory of their astonishment. "I'd have hated it if you couldn't have enjoyed it." After a momentary pause he grinned. "You were the belle of the ball, hon'."

She smiled. "Emily Upshaw wasn't competing. That means I outshone Mr. Wootton, and the lieutenant, and that Frenchman, and—"

"And all their dreams," Bryant cut in with a laugh. "You were like a tonic to them. I don't suppose most of them have seen anyone like you for half a lifetime, if ever."

"Now you're exaggerating, Mr. Bryant."

"Not at all, Mrs. Bryant." He felt a sudden rush of pride and pleasure in his young wife. She had indeed enchanted them all at supper. Even the drawn look left over from her illness heightened her beauty, making her appear more fragile than she was, her gray eyes even larger. He leaned over to brush his lips against her cheek. "You've won the West."

She laughed. "I still have a way to go."

For some reason that sobered him. When she noted his silence, she asked him what was wrong.

"Nothing to worry about. That is . . . it was something Lieutenant Cole said tonight."

She waited, sensing his reluctance.

"He's had a change of orders. They were waiting for him here, sent from Santa Fe. He's to stay here and wait for the arrival of other dragoons. There was another company supposed to leave Missouri a week after we did, under a Lieutenant Love, escorting pay for the troops at Santa Fe. They would have taken the cutoff we saw, and they must have traveled faster than we did. Anyway, they might be at Santa Fe now, Cole thinks, if they didn't meet any trouble."

"But we were to have an escort—they were to stay with the wagons to Santa Fe, to see us safe."

"I know."

After a brief silence she said, "What does it mean, Ter?"

"A few days delay, that's all. Mr. Bent says there's sure to be others traveling to Santa Fe soon. And he thinks that traders and troopers are certain to be going on to California. This won't stop us, hon', you can be sure of that."

She knew that he was not as much at ease in

his mind as he tried to sound. Suddenly the night air felt chill, and the sense of peace she had felt over the plains only a few moments ago was gone. It wasn't safe or tame at all, she thought, and a night of mint juleps and white tablecloths couldn't make it so.

"Mr. Mansfield is joining our caravan," Bryant said.

Jaine smiled in spite of her unease. As if Mr. Mansfield's pen and ink could make up for the loss of a company of armed dragoons! The smile faded, and she shivered.

"Are you cold?"

"A little," she murmured. "You wouldn't think it could turn so cool at night, when it's so hot in the day."

She linked one hand with his, pressing close to him as if for warmth. Ter freed his arm and placed it around her shoulders. She stared out once more at the prairie, a mysterious, alien landscape touched by the frosty light of the stars and the pale sliver of the moon, and once more she shivered, causing him to tighten the grip of his arm as he hugged her close.

THREE

Angus Haws rode away from Bent's Fort in the early morning, alone, heading for the smaller fort established at Pueblo a few years before by Jim Beckwourth. Located further upriver, at the very foot of the Rockies, El Pueblo had already become a summer haven for many of the free trappers who came down from the mountains in the spring. Haws felt restless in a way new to him. He knew that he wouldn't stay long at Pueblo—he got along little better with idle mountain men or Mexican gamblers than he did with the traders and Indians at Bent's Fort, meaning that in either place he kept to himself.

In his mind as he rode he carried a picture of the young woman from Natchez, as clear as if it were a painting he could take out and look at. He made no effort to think of her. She was simply *there,* like a fragment of a lively tune that won't go away.

Wo-Man, he thought. Woman. He couldn't remember ever seeing one like her, not even as a boy, not anywhere in his travels.

She came from a world he had never longed for, one to which he had given little thought, a world of drawing rooms and carriages and fancy dress balls and liveried servants, he supposed. Angus Haws lived in a world of isolation and privacy and absolute freedom, where he could shout if he felt a yell boiling out of him, bed down with the sky for a blanket if he felt like it, pick up and go any time he chose. He bowed to no man—never would. He took no orders. He stepped aside for neither man nor beast. In his life there was no place for porcelain dolls. If he had been a humorous man, he would have laughed at the notion.

In fact his humor had been foul even before the coming of the wagon caravan to Bent's Fort. His entire winter take of beaver plews, all that had been undamaged by the grizzly, had netted him less than two hundred dollars. Instead of a dollar a pound, which had seemed like stealing a year ago, Ceran St. Vrain had offered a dollar a plew—for pelts averaging one and a half pounds! He would only pay half price for some skins that bore talon marks. Haws had stamped out in rage, but the canny trader had been indifferent. Haws soon learned that he would get no more for his plews anywhere, even if he were willing to transport them all the way to the Platte River trading posts. After two days Haws had stalked into the long storage room where St. Vrain was tallying his goods for the caravan he was making up to take to St. Louis. "They're yours then," Haws said harshly.

"And those with scratchings?" St. Vrain asked coolly.

"Pay what you will," Haws said angrily.

Old Bill Williams was at the fort then. He was a loner like Haws, a throwback to the old days, one who wintered alone when he wasn't living in the village of his Ute wife, one who trapped beaver in secret streams and lost lakes high in the remotest mountains, one who appeared out of nowhere and soon went his own way again. His small eye pecked at Haws from his ducked head, and he said, in that peculiar squeaky voice that made it uncertain whether he was laughing or complaining, "Beaver's done, Haws. Damme if they's ary a place left for varmints like you and me. Them's gone under, what we shed tears for, they's fortunate they didn't hold up for such times as these." His bright glance pecked and shifted away. "Yessiree, you'd best do like me, hire on to keep these troopers from the States from gittin' lost, or shoot meat for the greenhorns. It's all that's left."

Haws grunted his disbelief.

"Don't like it no better'n you," Old Bill whined. "And I expect you wonders why this child don't jest set in the lodge an' let that Injun woman o' mine take keer o' me. Well, them damn Utes is makin' trouble, that's why! Old Bill's too long in the tooth and ornery to go on the warpath."

It was Williams who asked William Bent to take Haws on as a hunter for the summer, at a dollar a day, knowing how little the mountain man had got for his pelts. So Haws stayed around the fort for two months earning wages. It was easy pay. For a time he moved into a lodge with a Cheyenne squaw, but she was lazy and independent, spoiled by dealing with the traders at the fort, her greased hair crawling with graybacks, and the scraps that came out of her cooking pot were so bad that Haws took to eating in the employees dining hall at the fort, where the fare was much better. After a while he moved out, and slept thereafter alone in a stall overlooking the alley at the rear of the fort.

Having collected his pay, Haws was now heading for the mountains once more with his string of pack horses, his traps and gear, his small store of possibles. He felt relief, as if he had bolted out of harness. Even Bent's Fort was too crowded for him, too much like a giant mud chicken coop. Let Bill Williams scuttle and whine and scrape his shoes clean before he stepped over a doorsill. Not Haws.

Restless but relieved, glad to be out in the open prairie on no errand but his own, giving little concern to the danger of being surprised by warlike Utes or Pawnees or Comanches, pushed by a feeling almost like anger without fathoming it, Angus Haws turned his face toward the distant peaks, white with snow now in late July as they always were.

Every once in a while that strangely unsettling picture bobbed up before his mind's eye like an Indian's vision: a pale drawn face with soft gray eyes, framed by hair the color of old Spanish coins, the woman standing at the parapet of the fort in her white dress, as Haws had last seen her, himself invisible in the darkness of the veranda across the *placita*.

He rode on, scowling and angry and dangerous.

FOUR

The fight took place on the evening of the fourth day the Bryants had been at Bent's Fort. Ter Bryant never did learn for certain what had started it, but he guessed that it stemmed from an old enmity between Long Tom Brock and the buffalo hunter, Lucien Carpenter.

Bryant had stepped out for a stroll in the late afternoon, self-consciously wearing a new soft deerskin shirt he had traded for that day in the Cheyenne village across the river. Jaine was writing a letter home—a practice at which she was better and more devoted than he; for him pen scratching was worse than doing chores— and she had accepted the use of the desk William Bent offered her in his apartment, there being no furnishings whatever in their room but a straw mat for sleeping and a fireplace. Ter had brought a few things up to the room from their wagon, mostly a trunk of Jaine's personal effects and a small chest of his own, nothing to write on handily.

In his leathers, his face browned and toughened

from his weeks on the plains, his muscles taut and hard, Bryant was looking and feeling more and more like a Westerner. He longed to be back on the trail, an emotion he and most of the emigrants would have found incredible a few days ago. But travel had become a way of life, for the people as for their animals—even their stock ceased wandering far from the train after a few weeks along the trail. More than he had realized, Ter Bryant had come to relish being on the move, the motion itself and the excitement of the mornings, the great clamor and clattering and cursing until the mule teams were hitched up and set and everyone was ready, quiet coming over the waiting caravan until the captain's call rang out clear along the length of the train: "Roll 'em!" And the evenings, too, settling down under the open sky, welcoming that time of ease for aching muscles, hearing fragments of song from scattered fires and the endless talk of tomorrow and what it would bring. After four days of rest in Bent's Fort Bryant was itching to be on the move again, covering another fifteen miles on a good day, bringing their destination, the green valleys beyond the mountains, fifteen miles closer.

Absorbed in these thoughts, yet enjoying the feel of his new shirt against his skin, liking even the smell of it and smiling at Jaine's comment— "You smell like an Indian yourself, just like that giggling squaw!"—he made the rounds of the wagons drawn up outside the main gates, exchanging greetings and rumors with those he met. After a while he returned to the *placita* inside the fort, where activity had picked up late in the day as the sun went down. He was in the yard when he heard Lucien Carpenter's snarling challenge, heavy with a jeering taunt: "I'd as soon eat mule droppin's as set at the same table with you. Allus said you was dirt black all the way through. You got a nigguh's black heart under that nigguh skin, but you'll bleed white when this child opens you up."

Bryant saw Carpenter and Long Tom Brock confronting each other. Astonished at the vitriol pouring from the buffalo hunter's mouth, Bryant hurried toward the two men, joined by others who had heard the beginnings of the quarrel. Carpenter and Brock were at the south end of the courtyard. Soon the pressure of the gathering crowd was edging them back into the long alley that ran east and west between the apartments and the storage building that spanned most of the south end of the adobe fortress. That building projected beyond the apartment rectangle on the east side, forcing the outside wall to jut outward at that corner, breaking its straight line and creating a vacant triangle of space behind the eastern row of shops and stores. Here, largely hidden from the *placita* and out of the sight of any women or Easterners queasy over bloodshed, the two antagonists were urged and jostled by the crowd. Bryant heard men calling out, claiming one or another as his champion, and bets were quickly made on all sides as it became clear that a fight was in the offing.

Lucien Carpenter was almost a head shorter than Tom Brock, a bear of a man with huge arms and a great pot belly. His bushy black beard, hairy hands and tree-stump legs added to his bearlike appearance. He wore blackened, high-smelling leathers like the other buffalo hunters around the fort at the time. Bryant had not talked to him, but he had gained an impression of a surly temper and a disdain for the emigrants of the wagon caravan.

Only when he saw Carpenter's blade flash clear of its leather sheath did he realize what kind of a fight it was to be. His heart thudding, Bryant pressed closer, becoming part of a wall of spectators that, along with the adobe walls of the fort and its buildings, formed a ring at the center of which the two combatants faced each other.

All this while Lucien Carpenter's mouth continued to spill out its hatred, while Tom Brock remained stiff and silent. Bryant wondered how Tom could retain his dignity and apparent calm in the face of such epithets, which made his own anger rise. Only a whitening line around Brock's mouth revealed his anger.

"You run off from me oncet, like ary coyote,"

Carpenter said with a sneer, "but you hain't runnin' this time. This child claws like a grizzly, and he chews up coon for breakfast jist to get his jaws workin', and spits out the pieces cuz they hain't fitten to eat. You stole from me, Brock, and you cain't weasel outen it now. You stole and run, and I been waitin' for you to come back. Reckon you figgered it was safe now, ol' Lucien Carpenter would be long gone under and you could sneak back for seconds, but I hain't forgit and I been waitin' for the black to show."

"You be a liar," Long Tom Brock answered evenly. "And you talk like a scairt liar."

"I'll have your tongue for that!" Carpenter roared.

There was a loose board nearby, a plank from the adjoining carpenter's shop, between four and five feet long. Tom Brock kicked the board toward the center of the open ring and planted his left foot on one end. "Step on wood if you dare," he said, and the taunt was in his tone now. "First man to leave the board can crawl and eat dirt, or wriggle under it."

Carpenter seemed to hesitate, glaring at him. Then, accepting the challenge, he stepped onto the other end of the board. There was a sigh of expectation from the onlookers, followed by a sudden silence. The buffalo hunter lunged first, and the fight was on.

The two men were silent now, their clashing

69

blades taking up the quarrel. It was the crowd that yelled and cheered and groaned aloud, taking sides, shouting warning or encouragement. Caught up in the spectacle in spite of his fear for his friend's life, Ter Bryant shared the pounding excitement.

It was soon apparent that both fighters were experts with their knives. Lucien Carpenter wielded the familiar bowie knife, a long wide blade with a clipped point, curved and hollowed at the back. Bryant, who owned a similar knife— Colonel James Bowie's fame had earned him many young admirers in the South, a fame scarcely dimmed by the heroics at the Alamo— estimated the buffalo hunter's blade to be about twelve inches of razor-edged steel, with the three-inch hollow at the back sharpened to make it a two-edged weapon. It could chop and slash and rip as well as stab, and Bryant, though he had never had cause to use his own in a fight, had seen such knives employed with murderous effect on the Mississippi waterfront.

The short stabber Tom Brock carried seemed puny by comparison. Bryant had often noticed it, for Brock used it as a utility knife a dozen times a day. It sometimes hung around his neck from a thong laced through a hole in the bone handle. That thong was now wrapped around his wrist so the knife couldn't be dropped. Tom Brock called it a dag. He said that he took it off a dead Indian somewhere in the Northern Plains. He never said how the Indian came to go under. Indians, he said, had acquired such dags in trade from the northern fur companies. They were heavy enough to use as spear points or the heads of war clubs as well as knives. Brock's was a double-edged blade with a spear point, close to eight inches long and more than two inches broad at the heel. Bryant had found it an impressive knife, heavy enough to cut wood, but he wouldn't have wanted to carry it into a fight against a ten- or twelve-inch bowie.

Each man fought in a weaving crouch, his feet spread wide for balance, weight forward a little on the toes, the head and body held as far back as possible. Each knife reached out in front, held so that it pointed upward. Carpenter's great belly seemed a tempting target, his bulk ponderous, but like the bear he resembled he moved with deceptive speed, and every time Long Tom Brock's stabber went for the hanging pot it came up empty. The buffalo hunter used his bowie knife like a fencing master, catching Brock's blade and shunting it aside, striking back before Tom could leap out of reach.

True to their bargain, the fighters kept one foot on the board, though it was not always the same foot. They shifted nimbly this way and that, first one foot and then the other touching wood.

After a while the different styles of the two

fighters became distinguishable. Long Tom Brock arched and bowed his tall, limber body to keep it out of reach. He tried to take advantage of his longer arms to drive his short blade home. He used it in a straight-on stab toward that huge gut before him, or in a wide, sweeping, disemboweling stroke below. A few times he nicked cloth or drew blood from a shallow cut, but that was all.

Lucien Carpenter began to jeer at him. He had the better weapon, it seemed to all, and knew it. He was content to make the fight last a long time, not trying to end it with a lethal strike but using his long blade in flicking, whittling strokes at the nearest flesh that presented itself. With every exchange he left a ribbon of leather dangling on a sleeve or shoulder or extended thigh, and beneath it a rising welt of red. Within ten minutes Long Tom Brock had a score or more of cuts along both arms, across his shoulders, over his ribs and along his right leg, the one he usually kept slightly forward. Once, with an exulting laugh, Lucien Carpenter came near slicing off the tip of Brock's nose. The curving point missed its target but sliced across the Negro's cheek as his head twisted away.

"Waugh!" Carpenter roared. "Damme if he don't bleed like ary a man. I'm gonna serve up rattlesnake stew this night, ever' piece bite size!"

Like a brutal struggle in the dust of the pit, or

like the collision of two proud, long-antlered bucks pawing the snow and rattling the woods with the musket fire of their clashing horns, the fight seemed as elemental as the earth itself. Ter Bryant felt his own blood racing, his lips dry and his palms moist. He had lost all track of time. He was no longer able to tell how long the fight had lasted, certain only that every passing minute drained more of his friend's strength through another two, three, or four new cuts. Although the buffalo hunter seldom struck for Tom's head or ribs, preferring to find softer, more vulnerable flesh with the flicking edge of his knife, he had nicked off one ear lobe, and every time the Negro jumped or dodged, he sent a spray of bright red droplets flying. There was a continuous roaring in Ter Bryant's ears, and in his excitement he couldn't be sure if the sound was in his head or the voice of the crowd.

Then it happened—the first really telling blow was struck. Long Tom caught and parried one of Carpenter's strokes. Before attacking or withdrawing his knife hand, he hesitated for a fraction of a second. Carpenter struck downward with the back edge of his heavy blade, the blow almost like that of a club. The curve of steel caught the black man's knife hand. A piece of flesh flew out, like a lead bullet before a charge of blood—the tip of one of Tom Brock's fingers.

Ter Bryant felt a chill of fear. Time seemed to

stop. The loss of even a part of a finger of Tom's knife hand meant a weakened, unsure grip on a hilt now slick with sweat and blood. He saw Tom's wrist cord dangling loose as well, severed by the bowie blade in passing. The babble of shouts and the exploding "Waa-u-gh!" from the onlookers went up a notch in volume as they sensed the end.

Lucien Carpenter sensed it, too. His long knife darted and struck faster, more aggressively, trying to force Tom Brock back off the board. To make him quit? No, it wouldn't end there, Bryant thought. The buffalo hunter wouldn't let it stop there even if Long Tom would crawl, which he would never do. It would end only with that terrible blade plunged deep into the black man's heart.

Instinctively Ter Bryant lunged forward, not even knowing what he was doing. A powerful hand caught his arm and hauled him back. He found himself looking into Dick Wootton's grizzled face.

"Let go!" Bryant yelled. "He'll die!" The words were lost in the clamor of the crowd.

"You cain't!" the mountain man scolded him. "Best learn it now. A man's fight is his own. Try to interfere and they'll make flymeat o' you!"

Bryant let himself be held, knowing that Wootton was right, realizing that any attempt to jump into the fight would only shame Tom Brock without helping him. There was nothing he could do, nothing at all. He could only watch, helpless, as Lucien Carpenter cut up his friend at will.

Then a sudden, exploding roar of sound jerked his gaze back to the fighters. He gaped in astonishment.

Long Tom Brock had seemingly made the same mistake a second time. Parrying one of Carpenter's blows with his stabber, steel ringing loud on steel, he had been slow to withdraw his knife. The buffalo hunter's blade came down again in the same chopping backhand blow. The curving edge at the back of the point slammed down on Tom's upraised forearm, biting deep until it jarred on bone.

But in the same movement that brought his arm up defensively, Tom Brock flipped his dag from his right hand into his left. His right forearm twisted, the movement for a fleeting moment causing the flesh to bind and to grip the buffalo hunter's steel. In that instant Brock lunged forward. The buffalo hunter was held within reach. Tom's left hand drove his stabber into Carpenter's hanging belly.

"Up to Green River!" Ter Bryant heard his own exultant shout.

Lucien Carpenter's bellow of rage choked off. He lurched off the board, his mind in the face of death no longer able to hold any thoughts of honor, centered only on survival. He tried to reach Tom Brock's loins with a single crippling stroke from the side. He extended himself too far, and his deep wound had already slowed his reflexes. Before he could withdraw, Tom's dag struck down like the blow of an ax across the wrist of his knife hand.

The bowie knife spilled from Carpenter's hand. Slowly he sank to his knees. Suddenly the crowd was silent, as if a single voice had been cut off by a hand at its throat. All waited for the death blow.

It didn't come. Long Tom Brock looked down, swaying, at his crippled enemy. Then he turned on unsteady legs and stumbled away. The silent watchers parted to let him through.

Almost immediately Ter Bryant was at the black man's side. "Tom! My God, Tom . . ."

At first it seemed as if the tall man didn't know him. Then his eyes found Bryant's face and reason entered them. His teeth showed in a wide, slow grin. "This child . . ." he began. Then he sagged. Bryant caught him as he fell.

It was after he had helped to lift and carry Tom Brock over to the shelter of the veranda in front of the carpenter's shop, while someone brought cloths to stop various points of bleeding and one man ran toward the blacksmith's for a hot iron to use on the finger that had been severed at the top joint, it was there that Bryant's glance happened to lift toward the balcony across the way, outside of William Bent's apartment. From that elevation

76

an angle of view was offered across the alley toward the triangle where Brock and Carpenter had fought.

Jaine Bryant stood there, holding onto the railing, her face and lips as white as the dress she wore.

4 / Comanche Raid

ONE

It was a violent land. That was the one thing Jaine Bryant had not sufficiently understood. It was the thing against which some part of her—an important part—still cringed. And yet it was a thing that she must learn to live with, even to accept as normal, if she was going to make any kind of life in the Far West.

How could she hope that California would be any different? Hadn't it seen war and fighting this past year, the Bear Flag Revolt that had so excited Ter, and the triumph of General Kearny's Army of the West? Weren't they hoping to follow in the tracks of the Mormon Battalion? And didn't California have Indians? Didn't it have rough-hewn trappers and hunters? Didn't it have Mexicans like the ragged troupe that had joined the wagon caravan? Wasn't it a haven for adventurers of every kind?

As for the land itself, even when it did not threaten it was intimidating. The caravan was climbing steadily, the land heaving upward under their wheels and hoofs and feet, and the long-awaited mountains were close at hand. Their great tumbling flanks and soaring white peaks dwarfed the tiny wagons, making Jaine feel small and insignificant.

She had seen violence at home, and death, too. She had seen a runaway slave shot in the street, and witnessed many beatings and whippings of slaves. She'd seen men fight as well. She hadn't liked any of it, but such scenes had been on the periphery of her life, not at its center.

At first the Cheyenne Indians around the fort had frightened her, but after one or two peaceful walks through the village with Ter and others she had begun to feel more at ease. They were people after all, darker-skinned, hungry and dirty, evil-smelling at times (but so were many of the white hunters and traders), but people. Women with babies. Young children smiling and laughing. Fat old men and wizened old squaws. Young warriors puffed up with themselves, strutting and boasting, not unlike many a youthful Mississippi riverboat "warrior." Closer acquaintance, the perception of ordinary events in ordinary lives, the removal of mystery, all helped to banish fear. Jaine hadn't *liked* going among the Indians, but she had felt much less timid after a few days.

But knowledge of other Indian violence kept intruding on her, voiding any peace of mind. Someone at Bent's Fort had told a story of a white woman who had stumbled out of the arid wasteland to the south last summer, alive by some incredible chance after Comanches had attacked a wagon train, killed her husband, stolen her son and captured her. Somehow she had escaped and was found wandering in the waterless desert by a group of buffalo hunters, who brought her to the fort. Weeks later her son, also rescued by white hunters, was returned to the fort, where he appeared like an apparition to his startled mother in Bent's kitchen.

It was one of many such stories, for almost daily, it seemed, there was news of fresh Indian atrocities somewhere across the hostile Southern Plains.

The fort itself was not immune to violence. Two drunken dragoons had had a brutal fight in the center of the *placita*, after which one went swimming naked in the river and nearly drowned. Both were punished by having to march back and forth across the northern wall of the fort, carrying packs of sand. Such incidents were considered normal.

Worst of all to see was Tom Brock's duel with the huge buffalo hunter. The din of shouting spectators had reached Jaine Bryant in Bent's apartment, where she was writing a letter. It had drawn her out onto the balcony. She hadn't seen all of the fight—she could be glad of that— but she had seen too much. She'd heard Lucien Carpenter's anguished bellow at the end, like a death rattle. And she'd watched Tom Brock stagger away to be embraced by her husband, the Negro's leather shirt cut to ribbons, his body a river of sweat and the blood from countless wounds.

Jaine could hardly believe that Long Tom now rode with the wagon train as before, often scouting ahead because there were no dragoons riding point for the caravan. She could imagine the pain that must accompany every movement, but Tom gave no sign of it at all. With fresh clothes and less than a week's rest, he showed little evidence of that savage fight except for healing cuts in his cheek and at the tip of one ear. (He had lost part of one finger, Ter had said, but that was hidden by a glove.)

Even more remarkable had been the news that the buffalo hunter, Lucien Carpenter, would apparently survive. His ample sheath of belly flesh had prevented his worst wound, the one that brought the fight to an end, from reaching any vital organs of life. He would never pull a knife with his right hand, Ter had said grimly—sounding *glad*—but he would live.

Already she could see the change in Ter, the way his mind adjusted to accept violence and bloodshed, a life-and-death fight with knives or a caravan attacked by savages.

Was this only a man's world then, this awesome, violent wilderness? Could she ever adjust to it? Would they truly find some sheltered corner where they could build a house and raise a family and sleep at night in peace, without starting up fearfully at every sound?

Even reaching Santa Fe was no certainty. She could see that in the careful, quiet eyes of the mountain men riding with the caravan now, and in the nervous, fearful glances of the Mexican hunters toward the horizon.

The Mexicans were the reason the caravan was moving again. None of the emigrants had been anxious to risk this southern trail without an escort, but two days ago a band of ragged men had come to the river from the south on mules and ponies, some of them wounded, all exhausted and in panicky flight. They were *ciboleros*, Mexican buffalo hunters, armed chiefly with bows and arrows. They had been attacked at their work by a larger Pawnee war party. They had fled for their lives, abandoning their meat and supplies and hides to the *diablos rojos*, the red devils.

The Mexican hunters were not welcome at the fort. Bent and his traders and many of the mountain men still harbored anger and hostility from the winter fighting in which Charles Bent was murdered. But the *ciboleros* camped outside the fort and were unmolested there.

Someone—perhaps Captain Upshaw or William Bent himself—had perceived that the Mexican party was large enough to offer some advantage to the waiting caravan, since both groups wanted to reach Santa Fe. Bent, whose company did extensive business in Santa Fe and the valley of Taos, had then ordered or persuaded a number of his employees and some of the mountain men summering at the fort to add their guns and numbers to the caravan, along with a half-dozen freight wagons of the Bent-St. Vrain company.

A bargain had been struck. A dozen of Bent's traders and drivers, four mountain men and thirty-six of the Mexican hunters well enough to ride had been added to the caravan. It was now a company large enough to discourage any Indian war party, Ter Bryant had argued with more enthusiasm than knowledge, anxious to put Jaine's fears at rest. They had ample water for the desert crossing. And this first day's journey from the fort, though miserably hot and uncomfortable, toiling through sifting dust and barren sand hills where only the prickly cactus seemed able to retain its hold in the shifting ground, had been faster going than anyone had hoped.

A few more days, Jaine Bryant thought, head ducked and a scarf held before her nose and mouth as dust blew over the creaking wagon, dust that was already grit in her hair and eyes and stealing under her clothing. Just a few more days to Santa Fe.

She would not think beyond that.

TWO

In the evening the toiling freight wagons belonging to William Bent—at the head of the caravan because Bent's drivers were familiar with the route—crawled up a long incline through some sand hills and rumbled, one by one, out onto a verdant table. Waa-u-gh! Ahead of them, a bright thread of silver spilling over a shallow bed of rocks, was the Upper Purgatory.

Within an hour all of the wagons had been corraled near the bank of the river. The spirits of the entire caravan had lifted. Here was water, cottonwoods along the riverbank, gnarled *piñons* scattered over the foothills to the west. And thrusting above these were mountains, close enough to touch, receding tier on tier to distant, snow-capped peaks. Even the air was cool and fresh after the brutal heat of the arid crossing.

Tomorrow would begin the agony of climbing through Raton Pass with the wagons, but that was tomorrow. This night there was celebrating in the camp. The music of Mexican guitar vied with an emigrant's fiddle for attention in the cool softness of the evening. Old Bill Williams, one of the mountain men who had volunteered to accompany the caravan to Santa Fe, offered to down the entire contents of a gallon jug of Bent's Fort rum ($24 the gallon at the fort) and prove his sobriety afterward by walking the length of a wagon tongue without falling off. When no one took his bet he lifted the jug anyway.

Long Tom Brock, as had been his custom during the previous long weeks on the trail, joined Ter and Jaine Bryant at their cooking fire, easing himself slowly to the ground. Jaine glanced up from her campstool and said nothing. She filled a tin plate with a meaty gravy and bread brought from the fort. Tom accepted it with a silent nod, his calm eyes studying her without expression. She saw that he continued to wear a glove over his right hand even while eating, balancing his plate on his knee and mopping up gravy with bread in his left hand. All of his movements were somewhat stiff and careful, and Jaine couldn't help thinking of the myriad cuts hidden beneath his soft new leathers, wounds slowly healing or seeping against their bandages where they had been torn open by the day's activity.

What kind of a man was he, behind that impassive black face? A killer? A dangerous animal, like any other in this wilderness? How many times had that knife now hanging from a thong around his neck come up dripping red?

She looked away, her own recently eaten meal resting uncertainly in her stomach.

Ter Bryant frowned at her reaction. She wasn't herself yet, and it was plain that she was cool toward Tom Brock in a way she hadn't been before. Was it because of the fight?

His own reaction was quite different. He found himself admiring the tall Negro more than ever. Jaine ought to know better than to blame a man for doing what he had to do. If she couldn't forget what she saw, she should keep out of men's affairs.

Bryant talked idly with Tom Brock about the next day's crossing of the Raton Pass. "Is it as bad as they say?"

"*C'est vrai.* She be no place for wagon. Steep, too many rock." His shoulders and face pantomimed struggle; the pain in his eyes was real.

"We'll make it though." Ter glanced at Jaine. "The worst is over."

Brock shook his head. "*Non, mon ami.* The worst, she is always what must still be done."

There was a loud roar from Old Bill Williams somewhere up the line, answered by guffaws and catcalls. Bryant grinned. "You think they'll be any use tomorrow? If what you say is right, it's a little early to be cuttin' the wolf loose."

Brock's expression remained bland. "De wolf, she be back in de cage by sunup. By gar, you don't have to worry about that old wolf."

He had emptied his plate. Now, returning plate and cup, he murmured thanks, declining more coffee—a rare gesture on any plains caravan. Rising stiffly, Brock said good night, nodded toward the silent Jaine and moved away into the darkness.

Ter Bryant stared after him. He said, "You weren't very friendly."

"I'm sorry, Ter, I can't help it."

"You could try. What's wrong? You don't think Tom picked that fight, do you?"

"I don't know. It . . . doesn't make any difference."

"Then what does? A man has to defend himself, hon'." In that moment Ter Bryant thought of his father. He hadn't seen the fight that had broken Colin Bryant—he hadn't even been born then. But he'd heard of the fight, a familiar story in lower Natchez, for the man who had beaten the elder Bryant still lived in a mansion on the hill. In his childhood Ter Bryant had answered taunting reminders of that fight with his own fists. Colin Bryant hadn't. He had quit, kneeling at the feet of the man who had whipped him and begging for mercy. Remembering that story, Ter spoke more angrily than he had intended. "No man can let another make him back down, even if it means getting whipped."

"Even if it means getting killed?"

"Even if it means that."

"What if he has a wife and a family? Do they mean nothing? Does she mean nothing?"

"If he can't stand up for himself, he's no use to her."

"My God, Ter, do you know what you're saying? Is that all men are, that they have to fight like bucks on a hill just to prove which one is stronger or better with his horns—or a knife?"

"Sometimes," Ter retorted. "Sometimes, yes. Sometimes there isn't any other way. And out here in the West you'd better stop questioning it. Out here we have to learn how to survive, and do whatever that takes, and no man can do it by learning to curtsy, even if a woman can."

"Then maybe we'd have been better off to stay in Natchez!"

She turned her back on him, banging tin plates and cups noisily. Ter Bryant rose, glared at her unrelenting back, and stalked off.

In the darkness by the river his anger slowly cooled. Somewhere beyond the far bank an owl hooted plaintively. An answer came, some distance off to the left. After a moment a dark shape rose from the cottonwood directly across the way, lifted briefly against the night sky and wheeled off, plummeting out of sight with a flurry of wings.

"I don't give a hoot," Bryant muttered, and then smiled ruefully at his bad joke.

He could hardly expect Jaine to forget that brutal fight so soon when he couldn't shake the vivid memory himself. She needed time, that was all. They both did. The wilderness, everything about it, its men and its rivers, its deserts and its mountains, tested you in ways you had never met before. Jaine had stood up to it better than many up to now. Maybe there were things they would both have to learn about themselves and each other, and the learning wouldn't always be easy, not out here, where everything seemed to be larger than life size, even the way a man fought or drank his whiskey.

She knows it, too, he thought.

When he returned to the wagon he wasn't certain what to expect. He slid under his blankets beside her and she turned to him with a half sob, and spoke his name. He felt a rising heat, an instant need to match hers, a need to reclaim each other. In the dark they found their way back to the love that had brought them so far and would, Ter Bryant promised, take them wherever they wanted to go. Apologies were made and hushed, anger forgotten, promises whispered, caresses returned.

A little later, lying on his back with Jaine pressed close to him, her head against his shoulder, Ter Bryant smiled in the darkness and murmured, "Hoo, hoo!"

"What's that supposed to mean?" she asked, both teasing and curious.

"Maybe some day I'll tell you, woman, if you're good to me."

The two young lovers slept together for the last time. When they met again they would be two different people, each changed beyond all recognition.

THREE

The attack came just before dawn.

Many in the caravan were up while it was still dark, anxious to be under way and to assault the dreaded pass. The corral was broken up while the first gray light filtered across the low table beside the river. The wagons began to string out, Bent's six wagons in the van, pulling forward to make room for the long train to assemble. There was some milling confusion at the rear of the line, where young Jeremy Rhoads was acting as drover for the loose stock. Ter Bryant, his mule teams hitched up and ready, went back to lend a hand.

Only habit made him carry his pistol in his belt, his knife in its sheath. His rifle was in its scabbard beside the wagon seat.

The first alarm came while Bryant was walking past the last wagon. Dick Wootton rode back along the line to alert the emigrants. "Them damned Mex!" he called out in disgust. "They's lit out, ever' one of 'em."

"Why? What got into 'em?" an emigrant asked worriedly. "Is anythin' wrong?"

"They jist got close enough to smell home. Never mind, we'll bust through that pass 'fore ye know it, and nobody the worse fer not speakin' *Español*. Waugh!"

He galloped back toward the front of the caravan. Bryant looked after him thoughtfully.

He saw the mountain man trot past the lead wagon, preparing to scout ahead. Then Wootton swung around abruptly. He was too far away for Bryant to hear anything but a sharp yell. The grizzled oldster made an urgent sweeping motion of one arm over his head. Then he was digging his long rifle from its scabbard.

At that moment the Indians seemed to rise out of the ground itself. From behind rocks and riverbank or out of ground shadows they rose, as numerous as wheat in a field. A volley of arrows whirred through the air and showered down upon the strung-out line of wagons. A weird, blood-chilling screech ripped from what seemed to be a hundred savage throats.

As Ter Bryant turned to run toward his wagon, gunfire crackled—from which side he couldn't say. Redskinned figures clad only in breechclouts and war feathers ran forward, fired another round of arrows, and dropped to the ground. Some were already among the animals at the rear of the train. Bryant looked for Jeremy Rhoads and shouted when he failed to see the boy. "Take cover, Jeremy! Stay down!"

But he kept remembering that Jaine was alone. He had left her holding the reins of the wagon. She was alone and helpless to defend herself. He ran forward. An arrow plucked at his sleeve.

Then the second wave of Indians charged on horseback.

Ter Bryant could hardly believe the yelling and the din, the pounding of hoofs, the *crack!* and *pow!* of rifle fire, the wing-beat of arrows flying near, the thump of lead or steel or sharpened stone into wood and canvas—or resisting flesh. And—almost lost in all the rest of the uproar—the screaming of those wounded or simply terrified out of their wits.

He had almost reached his wagon when an Indian jumped to his feet some twenty yards away. Bryant was surprised to find his percussion pistol already in his hand. The redskin was fitting an arrow to his bow when Bryant fired. The savage made a round mouth of incredulity. Bow and arrow dribbled from his hands as he toppled.

An Indian on horseback rode by in a flurry of hoofbeats. Bryant saw a rifle leveled at him. He dove for the ground. He never heard that shot. There was a second rider behind the first, another and another behind them, some bent low behind their horses, hanging on by a heel and firing under the pony's neck. Others rode disdainfully erect. Bryant rolled frantically toward the rear wheel of his own wagon. He felt the solid rim of the wheel at his back and scrambled around behind it for cover.

As he loaded again and popped another cap into place, an arrow whacked into the sideboard directly over his head. He shouted at Jaine, praying that she could hear. "Jaine! Get inside! Stay down, hon'—stay under!"

There was a protected hollow behind the wagon seat, a shelter built by the previous owner, with double sideboards reinforced by sheet metal placed between the boards, hopefully designed to prevent the penetration of arrows or bullets that would pass easily through the ordinary wagon sides. Long ago he had instructed Jaine to huddle in this hole in the event of an attack. Had she reacted as they planned? Was she safe there now?

A whooping warrior, brandishing a tomahawk, got within ten yards of the wagon before Bryant dropped him with a shot. His hands were shaking and they seemed to have lost all normal skills, but somehow he kept measuring powder, popping another lead ball on top of the powder, securing the load. Percussion caps were magically in place, the gun fired, the procedure begun again without thought. The barrel of the gun was hot, black smoke was all around.

Through all this furor Bryant had no notion what was happening with the rest of the caravan. They had been caught strung out, stationary, without any momentum that might have helped them wheel back into a circle. Many of the mule teams had not been set, and Bryant imagined he could hear them thrashing around in loose harness or stampeding in panic.

And all of the best men were up front, he

thought, the mountain men and hardened traders, men who had fought Indians, who had been through all this before.

"Jaine!" he yelled once more, hoping for her answering cry, thinking that he heard it but not sure. He wriggled along the ground under the wagon, trying to reach the front where she could hear him better.

He thought of the Mexicans who had fled in the night, depriving the caravan of thirty-six defenders. Had they known this attack was coming? Had the Indians been watching when they left, content to allow the emptyhanded *ciboleros* to slip through their lines rather than give an alarm, preferring to hit the wagons laden with goods and mules and horses?

With anxiety he remembered Jeremy Rhoads. Where had he disappeared in the first frenzy of the attack? Had he been struck by that first hail of arrows?

A drumming of hoofs cut through the noise and smoke around Bryant. He had time only to look up before something struck the ground only inches from his shoulder. An Indian lance was suddenly buried deep, still quivering from the impact.

In an instant the warrior was back, leaping down from his horse. Bryant had just fired his pistol. There was no chance to reload. A coil of flesh and sinew exploded toward him as it landed. He saw a tomahawk flashing at the end of a muscular arm. Instinct made him use his pistol like a club. He smashed it against the upraised arm before it could strike, then lashed back in a second blow at the Indian's head.

The rest of the caravan was forgotten. He saw nothing, heard nothing but the naked savage under the wagon with him. Everything about the man registered clearly and vividly—the ripple of corded muscles, skin darkened to a coppery hue, a broad face streaked with daubs of paint, black hair from which sprouted a pair of feathers. And a deadly purpose in black eyes as the Indian launched himself at Bryant with his war club.

The blow grazed Ter Bryant's side as he flopped away from it. It seemed only a glancing hit but it felt as if his ribs had been crushed.

His bowie knife cleared its sheath as the redskin turned toward him again. It all happened in a blur of seconds, but every detail of the fight was clear to Bryant. The cramped space under the wagon caused the red man to strike the iron rim of a wheel when he tried to lift his tomahawk, a honed edge of stone thong-wrapped to the end of a decorated handle. That accident diverted his intended blow. Ter Bryant attacked with a sweeping stroke of his long-bladed knife.

He hadn't aimed at any vulnerable spot. His blow was blind, panicky, instinctive. But the Indian's own momentum brought him within reach. The sleek sharp curve near the tip of the bowie blade caught him at the base of the neck. Bryant had swung so hard that the steel hardly paused as it passed through.

Seeing the sudden slickness on his blade like paint, Ter Bryant thought of Jaine's shock and horror when she stood on the balcony at Bent's Fort and saw Tom Brock's thrust into Lucien Carpenter's belly.

His own belly cramping in revulsion, Bryant rolled clear as the Indian dropped dead beside him.

He retrieved his pistol and crawled out from under the wagon, thinking of Jaine again but with a new fear. What had happened to her? Where was she? Why hadn't she answered him?

Another horse rode near and Ter Bryant lifted his pistol. In time he recognized Long Tom Brock as the tall scout swung down on the run and ran to his side. "Stay down, lad!" Brock shouted. "Keep low or they'll have your topknot sure!"

He heard the warning but he had to know about Jaine. In one step he had reached the front of his wagon. There his glance was caught by a flash of blue.

It came from well beyond the wagon, perhaps twenty feet away on the far side. Jaine had been wearing blue that morning, a simple muslin dress that was her favorite for traveling. There matching blue ribbon attached to the plain white straw bonnet she had donned. The flash of blue that Ter Bryant saw was too small for a dress. It fluttered, and he saw that it was a strip of blue ribbon.

Danger forgotten, Bryant leaped from the wheel to the wagon seat. "Jaine!" he shouted. But the wagon was empty.

The sickness of fear welled up from his belly to his throat. His glance swept the surrounding area wildly.

He saw her. Thirty yards away, she was struggling in the arms of a redskin who was trying to drag her onto the back of his pony. In the moment Bryant saw them he succeeded, sweeping Jaine off her feet.

With an anguished yell Bryant jumped to the ground. He took only one lunging step before something chopped his legs from under him. He sprawled onto his face and chest. Whirling around, Ter saw Tom Brock, the only one near him, calmly shouldering his rifle and squeezing off a shot. An Indian standing behind a low hillock with bow and arrow aimed at Bryant skidded back as Brock's lead ball smashed into his chest. His arrow flew wild.

Ter Bryant knew what Brock had done, understood in a flash that the black man's action had saved his life, but his rage remained. Jaine was gone, vanishing over a lip of ground in the arms of the mounted warrior who had seized her.

Bryant came to his feet on the run toward the rear of the caravan, thinking only of pursuit and the need of a horse. But even in that grief-stricken moment he was dimly aware of changes in the scene around him. There was less noise, less confusion. He heard no savage yelps and only a scattering of rifle fire. No ponies hurtled past him as he ran. Suddenly he realized that there were no Indians in sight.

At the last wagon he stopped in his tracks.

Every mule, every horse was gone.

On the ground where he had been herding the stock when the raid began, Jeremy Rhoads lay on his back, his head turned at an odd angle. He had been scalped.

Bryant swung around as Long Tom Brock approached. Ter realized that he had heard Tom's footfall. A sudden, eerie silence had settled over the train, pierced only by a moan, a continuous sobbing, a single rising wail of anguish far up the line.

"They've got my wife," he said, hardly able to speak, his throat choked with emotion. "They've got Jaine."

FOUR

Captain Upshaw was unhurt and he had kept his head. Now, with the help of Uncle Dick Wootton and a Bent employee named Coughey, a head count was made. Including emigrants, traders, Bent's employees, the mountain men and the journalist, Mansfield, there had been forty-one able-bodied men with the caravan, not counting the thirty-six Mexican deserters. There were also five women and nine children. One emigrant wagon had stayed behind at the fort, along with two of the original traders' wagons.

The Indian raiders—identified by both Wootton and Tom Brock as Comanches—had killed four emigrants and wounded eleven other men, some seriously. Miraculously none of the women and children other than Jeremy Rhoads had been hit, but two were missing, a girl of thirteen named Mary Cadigan—and Jaine Bryant.

By the look of things the Indians had suffered few losses. There were only two bodies visible, one the man Bryant had killed under his wagon, but Tom Brock told him that the Indians carried their dead and wounded off with them whenever possible.

At the end of the count there were twenty-six men unhurt and capable of defending the wagons. Three of the boys included among the emigrant families were old enough to carry rifles. That made twenty-nine. Some of the wounded could also fight.

It wasn't enough. Not if the Comanches came back in the same numbers.

A corral was formed beside the bank of the *Purgatoire*. Sentries were posted all around. The remaining mules and horses were turned inside the circle.

Only then did a small search party assemble. For Ter Bryant the waiting seemed an eternity. It was less than an hour from the time the Indians struck.

The search party had to be small. The wagons couldn't be risked for the sake of two women who might already be dead. This latter opinion was not voiced aloud, but the sentiment was there, clear enough for Bryant to hear it, reasonable enough so that he couldn't object. Seven men set off on horseback from the river, following Indian sign toward the east. In addition to Ter Bryant and James Cadigan, Mary's father, there was the trader from the fort named Coughey, Long Tom Brock, and three mountain men—Wootton, Baptiste Cormier, and Old Bill Williams. Not many in number, Bryant thought dully, but impressive in appearance, bristling with hair and weapons. He was the greenest man among them. Even Jim Cadigan was older and more experienced.

Three or four different sets of tracks joined on a ridge about a mile east of the wagons. From these tracks the mountain men estimated that the total number of Comanches involved in the attack came to around seventy. The mules and horses stolen from the train were not with this retreating force, having been herded off toward the northeast by an unknown number of Indians.

"I'd say they wuz nearabouts of eighty o' them red devils," Dick Wootton said. "A right sizable war party."

"Were they after the mules and horses?" Bryant asked. Conversation helped to keep his mind off what Jaine must be enduring—and the guilt he carried for allowing her to be taken captive.

"Mebbe so," Old Bill Williams opined. "But a Comanch' ain't a Ute and he ain't a Cheyenne. He don't allus need a reason. Mebbe he jist wants to take a topknot or two, or count some coup, or mebbe he jist feels mean."

The opinion was hardly reassuring.

Comanches, Bryant thought. The very name struck terror into white hearts and minds fed on stories of atrocities and massacres, incredible feats of horsemanship, unrelenting ferocity. At times the Sioux, the Cheyennes, the Utes, Pawnees, Pueblos, and Arapahoes had all met and traded peacefully with the white men invading their traditional hunting lands. The Comanches seldom did. They remained an implacable enemy, treacherous, arrogant, and hostile.

He couldn't let himself think about what Comanche braves did to white women captives.

Tracking was easy until the sign vanished over a rocky table. Then there was an agonizing delay before Long Tom Brock signaled the discovery of tracks leading north. At the same time Cormier found sign heading southeast. The war party had divided.

A choice had to be made. Seven men were vulnerable enough in a body in hostile territory. Even Ter Bryant had to acknowledge the necessity of sticking together.

On Bill Williams's hunch the party followed the trail that led southeast.

The Comanches had made no effort to hide their tracks, apparently having no fear of being followed. Dick Wootton was uneasy over this. Though Tom Brock said nothing, Bryant sensed that he was also disturbed by the Comanches' movements. After a half-hour's steady riding Old Bill, who had taken the lead, claiming to know this country better than any man present, held up his hand. The searchers pulled up.

The trail led down a long, natural ramp toward broken terrain, tumbling sand hills that fell away to the north, a low, flat-topped mesa on the right rising out of bleak, treeless flats. Something about the situation disturbed the canny mountain men, and after a moment's narrow-eyed study Ter Bryant saw what it was.

They could not see beyond the curving wall of the mesa. The terrain behind the sand hills to the left of the trail offered equal opportunity for concealment. The Indians' tracks led between these unknowns. And the open flats at the bottom of the long incline were an ideal place for an ambush.

Old Bill Williams went forward silently on foot. In a few minutes he was running back, lurching awkwardly in that unsteady gait of his, as if he still felt the effects of last night's jug, though in fact the way of moving was natural to him. He vaulted into the saddle with surprising speed, wheeled about and called out sharply, "Ride, lads! Them heathens has played tricks with us. They's waitin' below, and dog me if we don't find that other bunch sneakin' in behind us. Ride!"

The other mountain men and Coughey needed no urging. They wrenched their horses around and started off on the run. Ter Bryant held his place, bathed in cold fear—not for himself but for Jaine. "I can't quit now!" he yelled. "Maybe it's not a trick—"

Dick Wootton skidded close, his face red. "Ye cain't help your missus by losin' yer own hair, lad. This hain't no guesswork—they's trapped us. Hightail it or we're done!"

For an instant longer Bryant hesitated, torn by conflicting alarms. The others were already retreating at full gallop, true to the mountain man's traditional code that allowed any man to make his own choice. The clear urgency at last cut through Bryant's reluctance to abandon the search. He set off after his companions. Old Bill Williams, the first to take alarm, veered away from their previous tracks, heading into a shallow gully that ran due north. The others followed, dust boiling up in a long snake to mark their run. As Ter Bryant saw the gully opening up, he heard a spine-curdling scream from dead ahead. An Indian on a spotted pony raced him to the opening of the gully, trying to cut him off. Dust rose behind him—a mass of it, Bryant saw, the sight freezing his mind so that for a moment he couldn't think clearly. Old Bill had been right. The second group of Comanches, after starting north, had circled back to pick up their trail, closing the gates of a trap.

An instant ahead of the plunging Comanche Ter Bryant reached the gully and raced along it, heels digging, his hat beating against his horse's flank. The horse, seeming to catch the panic of his rider, was in full gallop. Bryant heard a faint snapping behind him, like dry branches breaking, and knew it was gunfire. Through the whirl of wind and dust and pounding hoofs he heard the shrill yelping of the Indians taking up the chase.

Five minutes more and the gates would have closed, Ter Bryant thought as he rode. And for the sake of Jaine and Mary Cadigan six men besides himself would have gone under before their time. Yet they had not hesitated to make the attempt to rescue the two girls, and they must all have known the real danger they were courting better than he. They said that the mountain man was independent, that he wouldn't stop along the trail to pick up what another man had dropped to help him out. But he could be chivalrous, too, where a white woman was concerned, and he thought little of risking his topknot for a cause that struck his fancy.

Bryant had closed some of the distance between himself and Cadigan, the last of the six men ahead of him. And it seemed to him that his chestnut was outdistancing those Indian ponies, slowly pulling away.

The fleeing men emerged out of the cut onto a long, gradual slope that climbed toward the big bend of the Upper Purgatory where the wagons had been left. They were strung out in a loose line, pulling hard toward the clean edge of a ridge, when all of a sudden that horizon line fragmented. Before Bryant's startled gaze the specks of the broken line became larger, taking on the shapes of horses and riders. Horse soldiers! Belatedly the sharp call of a bugle floated down to him.

"Waugh!" Bill Williams yelled, and the other mountain men took up the exultant cry.

Behind them the dust of the Comanches, thick and wide, slowed and began to billow high, drifting ahead of the lead ponies. As the solid ranks of dragoons galloped down the hill in full charge, the Comanches turned and disappeared into the dust they had raised.

FIVE

"I'd like to oblige you, Mr. Bryant," Lieutenant John Love said. "There is nothing I'd rather have than a chance to hit back at the Comanche. But I have my orders, sir. I must follow them."

Love's dragoons had left Fort Leavenworth on June 8, escorting $350,000 in specie with which to pay the troops billeted at Santa Fe. In Kansas Territory the dragoons had been struck hard by Comanches, accounting for the lieutenant's bitterness toward these Indians. They had continued safely on to Santa Fe after beating off the attack. Accompanying them was Tom Fitzpatrick, the United States Government's newly appointed Indian Agent, who was with Love now en route to Bent's Fort near the end of a roundabout journey.

The horse soldiers had crossed Raton Pass early that morning. Descending to the level of the Upper Purgatory, they had discovered the frightened emigrants of the wagon train prepared for a siege. Hearing that a small search party had ridden after the Indians, Love had sent out a strong detachment of dragoons to their aid. Their timely appearance had, as Old Bill Williams

107

loudly proclaimed to everyone within earshot, saved "seven fine hanks o' hair from danglin' from Comanche belts."

Lieutenant Love had agreed to send a detachment of troops along with the wagons, seeing them safely through the pass before returning. That was as far as he would deviate from his orders.

It was what Ter Bryant had feared. Sick of heart, he turned away. "Ye done all ye could," Dick Wootton told him. Bryant hardly heard, angrily shrugging off any sympathy. He hadn't done enough. He could not forget how he had hit the ground when the shooting started that morning, instead of continuing to Jaine's side. He had saved his own neck at her expense.

The trackless desert in which the Comanches roamed without challenge stretched hundreds of miles to the east and south. Before a larger and stronger search party could be organized out of Santa Fe, the Comanche raiders would have vanished into that wilderness, carrying their two white captives, a thirteen-year-old girl and Jaine Bryant.

5 / *The Captives*

ONE

When the Indian savage dragged her from the seat of the wagon after Ter's rifle jammed on her, either through some mischance or her own ineptitude with firearms, Jaine Bryant experienced the terror of facing death.

Fifteen hours later, when full darkness at last brought a halt to her captors' punishing ride, she knew that she was not to be killed, that she belonged to the big-nosed leader who had carried her off on his pony, and she prayed for death.

They had stopped only once. Some time during the morning they waited behind a low mesa. The Indians took the precaution of binding her wrists with thongs and gagging her with a dirty wad of leather. The same was done to young Mary Cadigan, who cried constantly, inconsolable in her terror.

Jaine guessed that a search party must be near. The knowledge brought brief hope. As she watched the warlike preparations of the Comanches, saw them smiling and eager, she began to take account of their numbers. There were forty in the group remaining with her and Mary. Nearly as many more had separated from them some distance back. Hope faded. Instead she began to fear for the lives of any searchers, knowing that Ter would be among them. So many Indians would surely overwhelm them.

She wondered over and over what had happened to Ter and the others. When the attack started she had looked back to see him running toward the wagon. Then a dark-skinned savage, war paint giving him the look of some hellish apparition, rose from the ground to his left. She heard Ter's shot and saw the Indian fall.

In her relief she had had sense enough to crawl into the "fraidy-hole" behind the seat and crouch there. But Ter had not appeared. The screaming and shooting continued all around her. After a while she thought she heard Ter calling to her and lifted her head.

Instead of seeing Ter she had looked directly into the eyes of a mounted Indian facing the wagon.

The Comanche had approached from the far side of the wagon, away from the place where Ter had been shooting. As soon as he saw her he urged his pony toward the wagon. Too late Jaine dragged Ter's Plains rifle from its scabbard and tried to aim and shoot.

She dropped the rifle when it failed to fire and tried to scramble down from the seat. In the instant the Indian had seized her, clamping one hand over her mouth to smother her cries as he dragged her away.

She had almost managed to struggle free of his grip, because he was having trouble controlling his nervous pony while he tried to haul her onto the saddle before him. But he was incredibly strong and he soon overpowered her, even using one arm.

That was all she knew of the battle at the wagons. She had to believe that Ter was alive. Her sanity depended on it.

Suddenly the Comanches who had been hiding behind the mesa swept around the bend on their ponies. After a moment she heard their savage whoops and the sound of gunfire.

Only a pair of young braves had been left behind to watch the prisoners, and the two—they were really only boys, Jaine saw—were reluctant to be left out of the battle. They went forward to watch, and were soon ignoring their two white charges. Jaine tried to rouse Mary Cadigan from a state of near-collapse. With her mouth gagged, her hands tied, she had to kick the younger girl before she produced any reaction.

She tried to communicate with her eyes. *They're not watching us. We must run!*

Jaine glanced anxiously after the two young Comanches. One was already out of sight around the curving wall of the mesa. The other, on foot, had his back to her. She nudged Mary again with her foot and ran a few steps.

She looked back. With a muffled moan Mary Cadigan struggled to her feet. She had understood.

Jaine turned and ran. She heard Mary scrambling behind her. An instant later there was an angry shout.

The younger girl covered only a dozen stumbling yards before she fell. Jaine hesitated, looking back. The youth who had given the alarm ran past Mary toward her.

In desperation Jaine turned and tried to escape. Her feet sank into sand. Running with her hands tied was amazingly awkward, slowing her down. She stumbled into a clump of mesquite, raking her cheek. Pulling free, she tried to reach a dry wash, half heartedly hoping that she might be able to hide there.

Then she heard padded steps close behind. The young brave caught her by the arm and angrily threw her down. Her face was buried in sand. The grit filled her nose and she couldn't breathe. She began to choke and thrash around wildly.

The Comanche youth jerked the gag from her mouth. She sucked in air noisily, her chest heaving. After a moment she was able to sit up. She stared at the redskinned boy, who scowled down at her. Taking in a deep breath, she screamed as loudly as she could.

He slapped her. The blow was hard enough to cut off her cry and bring sudden tears. Then he jammed the wad of leather roughly into her mouth. He pawed some of the sand away from her nostrils and hauled her to her feet.

Alternately pushing and dragging her, forcing her to stay on her feet, the young warrior herded her back to the waiting ponies. The other sentry had easily caught Mary Cadigan.

When the main body of the war party returned, Jaine saw neither the grisly scalps nor the grinning triumph she had dreaded. Instead there was an air of haste and even fear. Rough orders were barked to the two young guards. The gags were removed and the captives' hands were freed. They were forced onto the backs of two ponies. When Jaine threw herself off the first time, she was forcibly lifted back up and her ankles were secured by a length of tough rawhide drawn under her pony's belly. If she fell off now she would be dragged.

The long journey began.

For hours the Comanches rode without stopping. They seemed tireless, indifferent to the bone-jarring miles. The land was empty, barren, as pitiless as the naked sun under which they traveled. Jaine Bryant lost all sense of time or distance. Only the slow crawl of the sun overhead marked the passage of hours. Her thighs were soon chafed raw from rubbing against the stiff leather saddle—hardly a saddle at all, but a leather blanket thrown over the pony's back and tied down. She settled into a kind of coma, her mind empty, her body wrapped in a dull cocoon of pain, her eyes burning from dust and glare.

In the early afternoon, at the peak of the day's heat, the Indians rested briefly beside a brackish water hole. One man tested the water and spat it out. The horses were permitted to drink, but neither the Indians nor their two captives were allowed water.

The warrior who had pulled Jaine from her wagon came over to stare at her in silence. From the way he had spoken, and the attitudes of the other Indians toward him, she had guessed that he was the leader of the raiders. He was a short, powerfully made man, bow-legged, his almost naked torso wide and flat. His eyes were jet black and expressionless, though she thought there must be curiosity behind his stare. His broad face, with its high cheekbones and powerful jaws, had a natural arrogance, an unmistakable pride. It was dominated by his prominent beak of a nose. Its wide, thick bone, curved like a talon, looked strong enough to break a fist, instead of the other way around. It had given him his name: Iron Nose. Complementing it was a mouth like a closed trap, wide and thin-lipped and, to her eyes, cruel.

Jaine made no attempt to repress a shudder.

Seeing it, his eyes were lit briefly by a flash of emotion, like lightning flickering against black thunderheads. He turned and stalked away. She knew she had angered him.

She also knew that she was *his* captive. He had claimed her for himself.

When the day began she was Ter Bryant's wife. Now, a prize of battle, she belonged to another.

TWO

Mary Cadigan died that night.

The Comanches did not stop until it was well after dark. Then they came to a river, its banks marked by a thin green line of cottonwoods and brush. The stream was wide and shallow, its current fairly strong. Though Jaine did not know it then, it was the North Fork of the Canadian.

The white captives were given water but not food.

The Indians seemed relaxed now, in good humor. They laughed and joked among themselves. They were able to look back at the morning's battle and boast of their deeds. They had suffered few losses. They had stolen many horses and mules, which had been driven ahead by a dozen braves and to which they had caught up late that morning. They had counted plenty coups. They had carried away two white women.

And even when great numbers of pony soldiers had appeared, they had escaped, leaving pursuit far behind.

For Iron Nose, who had planned and led the raid, it was a great personal victory. For all of his followers it had been a good day, one whose exploits they could carry back proudly to their own lodges.

Mary Cadigan remained subject to fits of uncontrollable weeping, and it was this that drew the attention of several young warriors. They grinned and laughed over the weakness and lack of spirit in the young white girl. She was of a poor age, too young to be a really useful slave, too old to be absorbed into the tribe as a true Ko-man-tsia. At last, after some consultation, three of the braves seized the girl and dragged her away. They disappeared among the brush along the riverbank.

Jaine Bryant jumped to her feet and started after them. Her angry cry was answered with laughter. Another man caught and held her. After a moment she sank tearfully to the ground.

A single scream shivered through the quiet night, as sharp as a knife edge. Then there was silence.

Jaine did not see the three warriors return. In the morning she noticed on two of the men portions of Mary's clothing. She couldn't bear to think in detail of the young girl's fate.

Yet, as the second day of her captivity wore on, she began to believe that Mary had been fortunate. At least her terror was over.

THREE

The journey lasted into the fourth day. Through that morning the contours of the land changed from the arid wasteland they had crossed to an equally desolate but strangely eroded terrain. Cracks and fissures appeared in the earth, widening until they became canyons. Towers rose thin against the sky like the spires of ancient cathedrals encrusted with stone. At first there were veins of red in the earth, then the dust itself became red. Weird shapes in red and brown stone heaved upward, pinnacles and buttes and massive piles of broken rock. Nothing at all seemed to grow over great portions of that vast wilderness, whose empty desolation, like the surface of some alien planet far from the earth she had known, threatened to crush Jaine Bryant's spirit. It seemed as if she had moved an unbridgeable distance from any place of ease or comfort or safety. This land was without mercy. Its people would be no different. They could not have survived in such a place if they were not equal to it.

Shortly after noon the Indian column rode

down a long, descending canyon trail. The gorge was so deep that the trail was soon in shadow. The crumbling walls closed in. Looking ahead, her eyes puffy and red from fatigue and strain and the inescapable glare of the sun, Jaine thought that her captors must have made some mistake, blundering into a box canyon. Then the stone walls parted as they came around a bend. The trail widened out onto a flat river valley. For the first time she saw the great channel of the Canadian, a river running wide and strong, muddy red in color, as if the water and the earth itself were drenched in blood.

Dotted along a section of the canyon floor was an Indian village, tipis clustered into a roughly drawn circle.

Women and children and old ones came out to greet the returning warriors. Barking dogs set up a clamor. The white woman was immediately an object of curiosity and fun. Young children and shrieking squaws ran alongside the pony on which she rode, some reaching out to pluck at her torn and dirty and bedraggled dress. Iron Nose rode up beside her and spoke sharply, driving the women away.

He led her to his lodge near the center of the village. It consisted of two tipis. The taller of these was not the largest in the village, but it was close to the center, taking second place only to the lodge of the old chief who came out to greet Iron Nose with evident pride and joy. Jaine Bryant sat unmoving on the back of the pony who had carried her so far. Hunched over, she was too exhausted to feel any new apprehension or even to try to pull away from the curious fingers that picked at her skirts and legs.

The old man was the peace chief of the village, as Iron Nose was the war chief. His name was Twisting Wind. He drew a few steps nearer to peer at the white captive. He shook his head. She was small and weak looking, so light that it seemed as if any good breeze might blow her away like the tumbleweed. Still, her ankles were trim. She sat in commendable silence. Her hair was a fine color, like the precious metal the white man coveted so much. If Iron Nose chose to take her for another wife, even though he had a good Comanche wife who cooked and sewed well and kept a clean tipi, the choice was his. He was the one who would have to keep peace in his own lodge.

In the afternoon the feast began in honor of the returning warriors and their great victory. The men gathered in the council lodge at the center of the village to smoke the pipe and to gain honor by recounting their exploits. There were drums beating and much singing in the village, the children played warlike games, the women were busy preparing food appropriate to such a celebration, cooking over open stone pits they used at this time of year, for it was too hot to maintain fires inside the tipis.

Jaine was taken into the larger of Iron Nose's two tipis and left there alone. She was too tired and despairing even to take stock of her surroundings. It was as if she had withdrawn deep into herself, her essential self kept remote and safe. Her body was something strangely separate from her. Nothing further that could be done to it could touch *her.* She listened to the sounds of the happy village and felt nothing.

Later—she did not know how much later, except that the sun was dropping behind a ridge to the west, shadows along the river valley were long, and in the connecting canyons it was already dark—three Comanche women came for her. They took her, unresisting, to the river. Her clothes were taken from her and she was permitted to bathe herself in the red water. Curious fingers combed the snarls from her long hair, which was left loose. Another woman came to the river's edge to watch, her expression sullen. After a while she went away. The others chatted cheerfully among themselves, laughingly matching their dark skins against the captive's, handling her without cruelty. She continued to hide within herself, her body a limp, inert envelope of flesh.

At length she was taken back to Iron Nose's lodge. The women anointed her skin with a musky oil whose perfume she found strong and unpleasant. Then she was clothed in a soft white deerskin dress laced along both sides and fringed at the bottom. When all was done she was left alone.

In the evening one of the women brought seared meat and water. She had seen the buffalo carcasses roasting over the fire pits, and the smell of cooking meat had grown stronger. She had intended to touch nothing, but her hunger overcame her resistance, and after the first bite she devoured the roast meat eagerly.

Through the early hours of night she listened to the celebration outside. It had lasted for hours, and now seemed noisier and livelier than ever. The drumbeats and chanting and the rhythmic sounds of dancing filled the soft night. In spite of herself Jaine had benefited from her bath, food, and rest. Perhaps to avoid facing what was to come—part of her mind knew why she had been bathed, dressed, and fed—she studied the tipi, which was dimly lit by starlight through a hole overhead and by the glow of fires outside.

The tipi was about twelve feet across, and much more comfortable than she had expected. Part of the cover had been lifted along the west side—the opening for a doorway faced east—to admit a cooling evening breeze, aided by the smoke flap vents near the top of the hide cover where the lodge poles met. She lay on a thick pallet of buffalo robes. A painted buffalo robe hung at the back of the tipi, Iron Nose's ceremonial robe. A shield decorated with the head of a buffalo in silhouette rested against the wall near the doorway. There were a few rawhide cases and pouches, and a large water bag, made of an animal skin or intestine. The hide cover of the tipi, creamy white on the outside, was darker on the inside, as if the hides had been smoked. The cover was tightly pegged and secured all around its base, except for the one lifted skirt, and there was an inner lining over the lower half. It was neat and clean and in many ways surprising. She wasn't sure what she had expected, only that her imagination had pictured something cruder, dirtier, less comfortable—less like a home.

A home.

Fresh panic made her heartbeat quicken. She fought it back, denied it, tried to hold herself remote and untouched inside her shell.

The drums and the singing were still going on in the village when the flaps over the doorway parted. They had been closed when she was left alone to signal that no one should enter. Crouching low to clear the opening, Iron Nose stepped inside. He adjusted the flaps of the doorway behind him, closing the door.

Sitting up, Jaine Bryant pushed back as far as she could against the far wall of the tipi. It was quite dark inside, although she could see the orange glow of fires against the single skins of the top half of the tipi, and there were a few stars visible through the smoke hole overhead.

She saw that Iron Nose had lowered the skirt along the west base of the cover, ensuring privacy. Oh please God, she prayed.

In the darkness Iron Nose came to her. He spoke in a surprisingly soft tone. After a moment he began to remove her deerskin dress. When she felt his hands on her, she discovered that her body was not something apart from her, an impersonal envelope in which she could remain withdrawn, inviolate. It was part of her, it was *her* body, and Ter Bryant was the only man who had ever seen it and caressed it and known it completely.

She began to fight with a silent, unyielding purpose. He was stronger than she was, much stronger, and after a time, when her raking fingers almost managed to reach his eyes, he became angry. He struck her, cutting her mouth, the blow so hard that for a moment she felt consciousness slipping away.

She fought until all strength was gone, and then she lay inert, sobbing softly, knowing at last that the life from which she had been so unexpectedly, cruelly wrenched was lost to her forever, that there could be no way back to that time of innocence and hope and untarnished love.

ONE

Deep in the mountains, far northwest of the headwaters of the Rio Grande del Norte, Angus Haws spent that fall and early winter trapping beaver, just as he had always done.

He had found a remote valley that seemed untouched by man. Even Haws had felt a breathless wonder when he first discovered it. It was his. No other human foot, certainly no white man's, had explored these streams and woods as he did now, or looked into the blue, clear depths of this mountain lake. No one could claim it from him. Here he would go his own way with no one to question or challenge him. After the dusty din of a summer on the prairie at Bent's Fort and El Pueblo, even the air was clearer and purer. The industrious beaver were plentiful, their pelts full and dense, although not as good as they would be in the spring after the cold winter months.

Even the climate in this sheltered valley was temperate in spite of the altitude. Often such remote valleys, at or above the timberline, enjoyed milder winters than the great parks much lower down, where the cutting winds blew unimpeded and the snowdrifts could bury a man.

Yet it was a season without pleasure for the mountain man. His mood remained dark. Perhaps it was shadowed by memory of the widening stream of emigrants and soldiers he had seen crossing the plains, clogging the rivers, denuding the prairie of its forage for their animals, filling the deep ruts cut by their iron wheels with their litter. And the air with their clamor of demands, rules, orders, manners. Perhaps it was embittered by the shriveling of the beaver trade, so drastically confirmed that spring by Ceran St. Vrain's hard bargaining, that made Haws's hard-won skills and labors in the icy waters of the mountains almost worthless. He still refused to accept any logical explanation for the decline of the trade. It was a trick, a scheme of the big companies to force the free trapper out of business, as they had done so often in the past.

And perhaps Haws missed Wo-Man more than he had first admitted.

Certainly he missed the snug warmth of the tipi. Like most white men, even the experienced trappers, he had never learned the trick of raising a tipi. Instead he put together a crude shelter whose skeleton was a crosshatch of bent poles, covered with buffalo hides. It gave protection from the worst winds as well as from rain and snow, but it was both leaky and drafty. With a fire going it was either too hot or too smoke-filled. Once it collapsed in a violent storm, and the loose-fitting cover was always tearing or pulling apart along his makeshift seams. Sewing and repairing such a cover was a squaw's work, not something Angus Haws could or would do well; Wo-Man had been expert at it. In her well-made tipis, pegged down tight, the skirts weighed down with stones, a fire always kept going in the pit at the center of the room for cooking and warmth, a barrier of brush and boughs set outside as added insulation against wind and snow in the coldest months, a skillfully engineered ground gutter ensuring that the floor was always dry, Haws had spent two surprisingly comfortable winters in the high mountains.

During those two years he had eaten better, too. Now he had fresh meat when he shot it, or the jerky he made and kept for the times when he was snowed in or could find no game. With Wo-Man there had been cakes and soups, the strings of wild turnips she saved for winter and used to flavor her stews, delicious themselves with a taste like mushrooms. And the tasty pemmican, a mixture of pounded jerky and berry pulp and suet, shaped and hardened and preserved in skin casings.

In addition to all that Wo-Man had repaired and cleaned his leather shirts and leggings, prepared softened skins for new clothes and made fine tough moccasins, collected wood for the fire, fleshed the pelts he brought in by patient scraping and set them out to dry on their circular willow hoops, and compliantly satisfied Haws's winter lusts.

He would buy himself another Indian squaw, he told himself. But he made no move. He would go down to Taos and move in with a brown-skinned, laughing woman from the south, he decided. No sense in freezing his tail through the depths of winter when the trapping was poor. But he did not go.

An Arapaho was best, he decided, meek and easygoing, like Wo-Man. He had enough pelts to trade for guns and trinkets and even a horse or mule, which he could then trade in turn for an Indian woman. Better that than give the plews away to greedy traders bent on keeping all the profit for themselves.

Or maybe he would find a slender-limbed Cheyenne girl, young, fawn-eyed.

Eyes like that woman at Bent's Fort.

Her image had lost detail as the months went by, becoming a kind of vision, like a woman in a dream, but he remembered those large gray eyes vividly, eyes that were anxious, not exactly timid or scared but not secure either.

Why should he remember her? She would be helpless, a creature like that, away from her house and servants. She wouldn't last out a single winter in these mountains without a slave or two to dress her and keep her skirts clear of the snow and wrap her in robes when the cold wind blew. What would she do in a cave or a lean-to or even a tipi? Let her burn her fingers on a hot stone and the tears would flow. Slap her once and there'd be more tears. Show her a mouse and she'd run shrieking. Show her blood and she'd fall into a swoon. Treat her like a woman and likely she'd break in two.

A woman like that wasn't real, Angus Haws told himself.

Yet she had come far.

Pampered all the way, he argued, scoffing at himself, by that dandy of a man of hers. Coughing and sickly and complaining of this and that, probably, and turning sharp-tongued when her young dandy didn't dance to her tune.

But the portrait was only half convincing. The other memory lingered, blurred now, like a vision born of the fever. It stayed with Haws until the first deep snows came. By then he had piled up a hundred pelts, enough for two full packs that would weigh out close to eighty pounds each. Haws was mildly surprised at doing so well, hardly aware that in his solitary life he had worked even harder than usual, burying needs and hungers in hard labor, not even sleeping as much as he might have in other times because his drafty shelter offered little comfort.

He reckoned that it must be December. A thaw came, predictably, melting away some of the deep snow.

He decided to go down.

When the decision had been made to leave this valley he had found, he looked upon it with a feeling of possessiveness. It was his. He wanted it to remain that way. He wanted to return to it and find it the same. The beaver were still plentiful. In the spring the trapping would be as good as it had been through the fall. He could look as far as the peaks and ridges permitted without seeing the smudge of a single fire. It was, in a way, a kingdom in which he reigned alone.

This was the only life Angus Haws had known since he was old enough to claim manhood. He couldn't believe that it must end, that the end had already come. He would come back and claim his place, and pit his skill and instincts against those of the beaver. He would trap and skin beaver as he had always done, and at night he would know the quiet freedom of the mountains. He wanted nothing else.

Except a woman.

Haws set about eradicating any evidence of his presence in the valley. His traps and personals he would take with him, but he decided to make a cache of some spare parts, tools and gear and to bury it. He destroyed his shelter, carting the long poles to a ravine where they would be lost at the bottom, soon buried under new snows. He used the hide cover for his cache, which he buried between two pines, on one of which he cut a small mark.

The winter snows would be his ally. Soon there would be no evidence at all that anyone had camped in the clearing.

Haws left the valley by way of a steep pass at its north end, following an old, narrow animal track. He had stumbled upon the gateway into the valley only by chance, even though he was searching for such hidden reaches. Another man might blunder upon it in the same way, but it seemed unlikely. Haws meant to leave nothing to guide him. The tracks he made as he left in the melting snow would soon disappear or be covered over. There would be no other sign to alert even the most cunning tracker.

From the height of the pass he had a last glimpse of the valley, still mantled in snow, the pine forest heavy with white shoulders, a crust of ice creeping away from the edges of the lake and the still waters formed by beaver dams, a thin mist like pale smoke hanging over the timbered slopes to the east and south and the steep bluffs to the west.

He turned away. He would continue north until it was safe to begin a wide circling that would eventually take him to familiar trails leading south.

South to Taos, then. And if he still wanted to, he would travel down to the Arkansas and find a Cheyenne village. He would pick a young girl this time, like the one he'd had in the summer of the flooding—that was in 1844. Blue Bird was her name. Not much for cooking or keeping a tipi clean—there had been mouse balls on the floor most of the time—but her flesh had been firm and pliant, and when Haws took her she had revealed hungers almost as strong as his own.

Trim ankles and arms, and eyes like a fawn.

Taos first, and if Old Bill Williams was there Haws would drink him under with Taos lightning, one kind of fire to quench another.

Thus it was that, in late December, Angus Haws came down from the mountain to buy a wife.

TWO

After their scrape with the Comanches, and after hearing hair-raising tales of the hazards and difficulties of the Old Spanish Trail from Santa Fe to California, no one with the Upshaw train, including Cal Upshaw himself, was eager to push on immediately. The previous winter Captain Philip St. George Cooke had led the Mormon Battalion to California, with orders to make a wagon road from Santa Fe. He had struggled through, but what was known of the ordeal was not encouraging.

There was still gossip, too, about the past winter's Donner disaster, grim news that had been only an early rumor to those who had spent the summer traveling across the plains, although Ter Bryant had heard some of the talk at Bent's Fort.

The result was that most of those who had made up the caravan professed themselves happy to stay in the new Mexican Territory, at least for the winter. There was some vague talk of organizing or joining a larger caravan to try the California trail the following spring, when they were rested and more was known of the dangers.

For Ter Bryant such talk only increased his bitterness. He no longer cared about the California dream. Without Jaine it was empty. All that was left to him was the guilt of knowing that he had brought her into this wilderness and failed to protect her. That he was alive and safe only added to his guilt.

Three days after the caravan's safe arrival at Santa Fe a large search party set out. Included in it were Cal Upshaw and several others from the train, along with a group of summer-idle mountain men and other volunteers. Ter Bryant was glad to have Long Tom Brock along with him as well, even though Tom was not yet fully recovered from his knife wounds. All told there were twenty-eight in the party, a group made formidable by the presence of so many skilled Indian fighters and trackers.

They returned to the site of the attack on the train and struck east from there along the trail the Comanches had taken. Late in the afternoon of the second day east of the Purgatory the Indian camp on the North Fork of the Canadian River was found. Nearby the naked body of Mary Cadigan was discovered in brush along the riverbank. They tried to keep James Cadigan away from the body, which had been mutilated by scavengers as well as the Indians, but he turned wild in his grief and would have fought them all. His anguished cries made all of the men turn away, but they struck most deeply into the heart of Ter Bryant.

But Jaine was not found.

For days the searchers struck deeper into hostile Indian territory. By then the trail was turning cold, and at last it was lost in a conflicting pattern of many Indian trails crisscrossing the Godforsaken land.

At the end of a week the pursuit had become blind and hopeless. A council was held at the night camp. Reluctantly a consensus was reached. The desert was too vast. There were too many holes into which the Comanches could have dropped. There were hundreds of miles to the east and south beyond the Canadian cliffs into the uncharted wilderness of the Llano Estacado, the Staked Plains. Moreover, there was now Indian sign all around the search party. None of the men shrank from a fight, but the old-timers among them had not lived so long in the wilderness by taking foolish risks.

"She's alive, lad," Uncle Dick Wootton told Ter Bryant. "Ye can be sure of that. And ye'll have word of her in time, dog me if ye won't. Sometimes an Injun will treat a white woman tolerable, if one of 'em taken a shine to her . . ." He broke off, seeing the bleak horror in Ter Bryant's eyes.

In the morning, it was agreed, they would turn back.

Through the night Ter Bryant lay sleepless. Before dawn he had made his decision. He sought out Tom Brock and touched his shoulder lightly. The tall man was awake instantly. "I'm going on, Tom," Bryant said. "I can't give it up. You can tell the others."

Long Tom nodded silently. Without a word he rolled out of his blanket.

"I'm not asking you to come."

"You can't do it alone, lad. You wouldn't last a week."

They caught up their horses from the picket line and saddled them, working in silence. If any of the sleeping men noticed—and Bryant was sure they were all light sleepers—they gave no sign.

A man had to make his own decision, go his own way; it was a code they all recognized.

As they walked their horses away from the edge of the camp they were joined by a third man. For a moment Ter Bryant didn't recognize him in the darkness. Then he nodded. James Cadigan had a right to go along.

THREE

One night, near the end of the first month of his long search, Ter Bryant crouched with his two companions on a ridge overlooking Mustang Creek. They were watching the distant camp of a small party of Indians, numbering seven or eight.

"They's Comanch', right enough," Tom Brock murmured.

It was a hunting party, armed with rifles. The sound of shooting had drawn the three searchers. The Comanches had killed several buffaloes. They had spent the late afternoon skinning and butchering the beasts, packing everything—meat, hoofs, horns, and innards—in the fresh hides. They were some distance from their village, for normally the hunters left such butchering to squaws. Here their work kept them busy until dark, when they camped near the creek.

By this time, the end of August in 1847, Ter Bryant was hardly recognizable as the young man who had set out from Santa Fe with the larger search party. He had not shaved, and a month's growth had produced a black, bristly beard. His buckskin shirt, new at Bent's Fort, was dark with stains and weathering. His face was leaner, darker, more mature. He had acquired a habit of speaking more slowly and economically, often looking off into the distance while he weighed a question before answering. The habit of distance was in his eyes, a mark of the vastness of this land.

Bryant's body had continued to adapt to life on the plains, where he spent most of his day in the saddle and lived on a diet of game, occasionally spiced by such treats as the pemmican the searchers had been given when they visited a friendly Pawnee village a week before—friendly, Tom Brock had surmised, because most of the fighting men of the village were away. Bryant had also gained increasing confidence in his skill with his Hawken rifle, a .53-caliber percussion rifle with a heavy 34-inch barrel. A hunter since childhood, Bryant had never before had to kill in order to survive, but he had brought down his first buffalo with one shot while both he and the animal were on the run. It had been a lucky shot, Tom Brock had said, but luck was "near as impawtint as a good eye."

In much the same way James Cadigan had visibly hardened during the search. Sometimes

Bryant wondered at Cadigan's persistence. His wife was safe in Santa Fe, waiting for him. But Mary had been their only child, and Cadigan was pushed by an emotion akin to but different from Bryant's, and perhaps even stronger—not desperate hope, but hatred. His determination to find his daughter's murderers had become an obsession.

From an old man in the Pawnee village Tom Brock had learned of a large party of Comanches seen in the region. During the ensuing week the searchers had cast back and forth, fruitlessly trying to cut sign of this group. The buffalo hunters now camped below them by the creek were the first they had seen.

"We can hit 'em when it's dark enough," Cadigan said now.

Tom Brock shook his head slowly. "They's done us no harm."

"They've done *you* no harm," Cadigan answered harshly.

Brock shrugged. He was a patient man, and he understood. "It be best to leave 'em alone. We can foller 'em. They might show us where de village be."

When it was too dark to see anything of the Indian camp clearly the three men cautiously withdrew. On the ridge they were too exposed—to wind, to dust, to Indian lookouts.

Their horses had been left in a draw below the

ridge. Mounting them, they followed the draw a short distance to the northeast, moving at a walk away from the Indian camp, making no noise. After a while the walls of the draw dwindled away, bottoming out near a bend in the creek some distance below the Comanches. There they made cold camp.

The sky was overcast, showing only occasional patches of dark blue pierced by stars. A wind picked up, cold and stinging with sand. Ter Bryant's sleep was uneasy. The wind whisper in the hollows of the plain, in the cedar brakes and among the brush and cottonwoods along the creek bottom, unnerved him, as if he heard not the wind but the soft scrape of a moccasin along the sand.

Some time in the night he woke suddenly. He was not sure what had startled him. He looked around for Tom Brock and Jim Cadigan. There was only one long shape on the ground nearby.

Cadigan was gone.

Then, clearly, from upriver, Bryant heard the crack of a rifle.

Long Tom Brock was on his feet at the same time as Bryant. "*Sacre bleu*! Damme if that *papa* ain't gone after them Injuns hisself. This child knew he had it in his head. I should've stopped him."

"We've got to help him, Tom. He'll get scalped for sure."

"We be all of us short of hair before it's done," Brock grumbled.

But the black man was already starting upriver, carrying his rifle, his bullet pouch and powder horn slung over his shoulder. He trotted steadily and made little noise. Scrambling after him, Bryant called out hoarsely, "Maybe we should saddle up. Time we get there on foot he'll be gone under."

"It be dark enough, they might not catch him quick," Tom Brock answered calmly, not breaking stride. "They's certain sure to hear us if we comes gallopin'."

The overcast night was black as a mourning coat. Brock had veered close to the water's edge along the creek bottom to avoid brush and twigs, running silently on the wet sand in his moccasined feet. Bryant, who also wore moccasins now, followed in his steps. It was impossible to see much of anything except the lighter shine of the water and the deeper black of trees and dense brush.

While they ran there had been some shrill cries and a few scattered shots. Suddenly they heard the drumming of hoofbeats heading toward them. The almost indistinguishable shape of a horse and rider hurtled over a hump above the creek and exploded through brush. Behind him a rifle crashed, close enough for Ter Bryant to see the spurt of flame from the powder charge.

The running horse went down with a frightened scream, floundering along the creek bottom. Bryant thought he saw the rider hurtling through the air, and he heard a splash, but in the darkness he couldn't be sure what shapes were real or solid.

"Waugh!" Tom Brock yelled. "Give 'em hell, lad!"

Bryant saw Tom drop to his knees and fire as the pursuing Comanches topped the sand hillock above the creek. Bryant did the same, shooting more at sound than shape. The fight quickly became a confused babble of savage cries and exploding gunfire. Horses and men blundered around blindly. Bryant delayed one shot for fear of hitting Brock or Cadigan. Someone splashed into the creek, and he caught a glimpse of a horse and rider plunging into the water after the man on foot. Then he had to duck as another rider almost rode him down. He brought his rifle up and fired as the Comanche went by.

Then a terrible scream rent the night, dying in a pitiful gurgle.

Trying to reload, fumbling for lead bullet and powder by feel alone, Ter Bryant sensed movement above him. He looked up as a compact shape leaped toward him. Instinct made him swing the long, heavy barrel of his Hawken rifle like a club. It struck flesh and bone a solid blow. The attacker fell away.

Bryant crawled into the brush. He had lost the makings of his load. There was more noise nearby, and as he turned to meet new danger something struck his head a heavy, glancing blow. He went down. The blackness of the night was on fire. He waited helpless for the final impact of tomahawk or lance or bullet, knowing that he was lost. The crack of another shot seemed far away.

Something heavy fell across his legs. Painfully he struggled free of it. Then, blind with pain and dizziness, the ground rocking under him, he crawled deeper into the brush along the bank of the creek, like a wounded animal seeking cover. He kept going until the strength oozed out of him in a rush.

The din of battle receded swiftly, and the blackness closed down like the lid of a coffin.

FOUR

Ter Bryant woke to smothering darkness, and to panic. He tried to move. There was a weight over his head and shoulders, solid yet soft. It shifted slowly.

In a convulsion of fear he heaved upward. The weight fell away. Sunlight burst upon his eyes, filtered through the sand that clung to his eyelashes. Still frantic, he pawed the sand away.

Pain lurched like something alive inside his skull. A wave of dizziness brought nausea.

He sagged back against the sandy bank of the creek, dislodging another soft portion of the bank.

It had saved his life.

Gingerly he touched a soft, spongy area at the back of his head. He found a lump. Dried blood coated with sand. Something had struck him from above, an Indian war club, he guessed. There had been a shot. Then he had tried to crawl away. The portion of sandy bank where he had lain was topped by brush, but the ground itself was soft and crumbling. A portion of the lip had fallen across his legs. He could see his path now. He had wormed free of one small avalanche, struggling on for another ten or twelve feet. There he had been half buried by another fall of sand.

In the darkness the Comanches hadn't found him.

They had found Jim Cadigan. His mutilated body lay at the edge of the creek, the legs sprawled wide and lying in the water. Bryant saw missing fingers and a bloody patch of skull where the scalp had been ripped away. His belly cramped and he turned aside, dry heaving, fighting back sickness.

Tom Brock too, he thought. They must have done Tom in.

The sun's low placement told him that it was

early morning. Flies buzzed around him and crawled over Cadigan's body. Ground mist still hung in pockets over the creek and the nearby sand hills. The air was still cool and moist. The sun hung beneath a long bank of clouds that reached out almost to the horizon. Those clouds had kept the night dark, he thought, helping to hide him from the Comanches.

He could not see his rifle anywhere along the creek bottom. Unless it was hidden in the brush, which seemed unlikely, the Indians had found and taken it. But he still had his knife and his horse pistol, powder and lead balls. He wasn't finished yet.

When the sickness and dizziness began to ease, he thought of looking for Tom Brock's body. Then their horses. With luck the Comanches might not have ranged that far downriver to find the horses.

Nearby a waist-high rock shelf offered a solid shoulder to the creek bank. Bryant struggled to his feet, stood swaying a moment for his head to clear, and dragged himself over to the shelf. After a moment's rest he heaved himself onto it. The smooth stone was split into several big chunks. When Bryant tried to stand up, his foot slipped. It skidded into the hollow between two large slabs.

Too late he heard the hard rattle of warning. Then something as solid as a thrown lance struck his leg.

He couldn't believe the pain. It rocketed through his body and exploded against the top of his skull. His hair seemed to stand on end, and his body was alternately bathed in hot and cold. With a strangled cry he collapsed across the low rock shelf.

The young rattlesnake, surprised in its hollow, dropped to the sand below after striking. Lying rigid, Ter Bryant stared down at the snake as it writhed across the sandy bottom. Nothing that small could hit so hard, he thought.

A chill grabbed his body and shook it.

He heard slithering movement behind him. Despair came. He couldn't move. His luck had run out.

But then there was anger, and with it the need to die fighting. With fingers that were thick and clumsy he tried to drag his pistol clear. He rolled over onto his belly to face the new threat.

A dark face lifted over the edge of the table. "Quiet, lad," Long Tom Brock hissed. "They's not gone. They be sure to hear you."

Relief and joy momentarily washed away Bryant's pain like a cleansing force. He reached out to grasp his friend's hand. "Tom! I thought sure you were wolf meat by now. Like Cadigan . . ."

Tom Brock nodded. "I reckon he was satisfied, long as he taken two or three Comanches under with him." The scout peered along the creek bottom toward Cadigan's body. "I feared you was caught, same as him. When I sees you down, and them Injuns whoopin' and hollerin' and hittin' at everything that moved, I went into the water. They didn't see me, and I swum like a fish downstream, and hid out on the far bank, like you done here. It's luck they didn't step on you, lad," he added.

"I know. Tom, I been . . . bit by a rattle-snake."

"*Merde* . . ." Tom Brock looked at Bryant's leg where he gripped it. He was sweating now, holding onto the leg hard as if to shut off the poison. "Where's the varmint?"

Bryant nodded toward the creek bottom. Tom Brock eased past him off the rock ledge, drawing his heavy dag. Dropping to the sand, he disappeared from Bryant's view along the bottom. Then his knife flashed high for an instant.

Seconds later Long Tom reappeared, wiping his stabber on his shirt sleeve. When it was thus cleansed, he used the blade to part the cloth over Bryant's calf. Tom grunted. "Set your teeth, lad. Got to bleed some of that poison out."

Bryant's leg muscles quivered as Tom Brock's knife opened the wound. He took one glance at the green mass that spurted out of the already swelling calf along with the blood before he lay back, eyes squeezed shut, his fingers biting into his palms.

After what seemed like a long while, Tom Brock said, "Powder's best for rattlesnake bite. If you're to walk again lad, we has to burn it clean now. Jist don't go callin' them Injuns to come watch."

Bryant lifted his head to watch his friend pour powder into the cup of his palm, a small measure. Another chill shook him and he dropped back again, stiffening as he felt the powder charge poured into the open wound. To keep his mind from dwelling on what was coming he talked, the words jerking out of him in short spurts. "That was . . . such a little snake, Tom. You wouldn't think . . . it could carry so much . . . poison."

"Don't make no matter how big she be, when it comes to rattlers. A young one, she carry the same poison as the old. She's born with it."

Bryant heard the scratch of Brock's flint. It took several tries before the sparks ignited the powder in a small, hissing explosion. Bryant's body arched high off the rock, only his heels and shoulders touching. He collapsed, trembling, dimly aware of pride that he had made no sound.

After a time, when Brock had moved him from the top of the rock shelf into the shade of a nearby cottonwood, the scout said, "You has to rest a day or two 'fore you can walk out of here. But walk you will, lad. You did fine."

"I can ride."

Tom Brock shook his head sadly. "This child

147

sneaked downriver 'fore he come lookin' for you. Them Comanches must've figgered they'd be more than one horse close by. They stole ours, boy. We be on foot now."

"My God!"

Long Tom answered with one of his rare, full smiles. "*Oui, oui. Mon Dieu*. If you's good at praying, lad, this be a fine time for it."

FIVE

On the third day Ter Bryant insisted that he could walk. The Comanches had left on the first day after the skirmish, luckily not returning to the creek to search for any survivors, happy with one scalp and three horses to show for the encounter. "Be a great victory, time they gits home," Tom Brock commented.

Sixty or seventy miles of open, desolate, sun-parched wilderness lay between the two men and the Arkansas to the north. They set off at first light, rested at noon, and by late afternoon had crossed Beaver Creek. There they made camp.

In all that day, and the next, they saw nothing alive on the desert, animal or human. It was the land itself that threatened them, assaulting the mind with its vast, indifferent emptiness. By the end of the second day's march Bryant's leg had swollen up again and he was limping badly.

He walked with the aid of a stick Brock had cut for him to use as a cane.

Before nightfall they reached the Cimarron. The river looked dry at first glance, but in its bed they found small, shallow puddles. Tom Brock scooped out sand to a depth of six inches. They watched the hole slowly fill with water. In the morning they would fill their canteens with water for the grueling stretch of desert that faced them, fifty miles or more without water.

That night they talked of waiting where they were, sitting beside the dusty tracks that marked the Cimarron Cutoff, leading northeast toward the Arkansas, southwest toward Santa Fe. But the Indian menace had made traffic light all that summer. They might wait a week or more without seeing wagon or soldier.

Too long to sit in hostile territory, two men afoot with only one rifle and a pistol between them.

By morning Bryant had come down with a fever. For another day and night they rested in shade by the nearly dry riverbed. In the middle of the following day the fever broke.

That night Ter Bryant slept comfortably. He had been able to keep his evening meal down—it was the last of their fresh meat—and he vowed that he would be walking out ahead of Tom Brock in the morning. His dreams were hardly different from those that had come in the delirium of his fever: he dreamed of Jaine.

She was never far from his thoughts, waking or sleeping, nor would she be during the remainder of this desert ordeal. For somewhere in this same hostile wilderness she was a captive, at the mercy of a Comanche warrior, more helpless than he was, more lost, even more alone.

The friendship he felt toward Long Tom Brock deepened with each passing day, each plodding mile across the sandy wastes. Not once had Brock apparently given any thought to striking out on his own, unhindered by a partner who was half-crippled and weakened by pain and fever. They never spoke of that or of the bond between them, but it was there, needing no voice.

The long walk from the Cimarron to the Arkansas took four days. Bryant guessed that he would have become hopelessly lost on his own, for there were no clear trails to follow that struck directly north. Brock plotted their course by sun and stars without hesitation, as if he were out for a Sunday stroll.

During their noon camp on the third of these days they shared the last drops of water. From there they went dry. For much of the last day—Bryant never knew how far, for distances had lost meaning—Tom Brock carried him.

The sun hung low above the western sand hills in the early evening of the fourth day from the Cimarron when Tom Brock, leaving Bryant to rest briefly, walked to the top of a sandy mound.

He stood tall against the sky, and Ter Bryant heard his soft exclamation. "Waugh! There she be, lad! There be the Arkansas!"

Bryant struggled to his feet and hobbled up the low rise. He stopped beside Brock, swaying, tears making him blink.

Below them, colors muted in the setting sun, were the tipis of a Cheyenne village grouped along the south bank of the river. For long minutes they stood silent, drinking in the sight of the river's long, twisting line as if they could already taste the water. "That's some," Bryant said at last, borrowing one of the mountain man's phrases. "Yessiree, that's some."

SIX

After he had kept the white woman in his main tipi for a month, Iron Nose decided in disgust that she was no fit wife for a warrior like himself. There was only hate in her eyes. There was no laughter in her heart. When he came to her in the night it was like lying alone on the sand. She remained lifeless, cold, unresponsive. Even when he beat her she did not react. She lay inert, or sat with her shoulders hunched over and her head bent under the blow, making no sound at all. At such times Iron Nose sensed a contest of wills, and sometimes this enraged him, causing him to redouble the force and frequency of his blows until he succeeded in wrenching from her a cry of pain.

He had soon discovered that she was inept in other duties of a woman. She could neither cook nor keep a good fire going nor perform well the skilled arts of treating hides or sewing or beadwork. All she was fit for were things that a child could perform, or the lowest slave, such as carrying water or gathering broomwood for kindling or sweeping the floor of the tipi.

These failings were not of great moment, for Iron Nose still had his first wife, Standing Owl, to care for him, along with her sister and her mother. Since he had brought the white woman to his lodge, Standing Owl had been relegated to the second of his tipis, the smaller one, which she shared with their son and her sister and parents, leaving the privacy of the large tipi to Iron Nose and the captive. During this time Standing Owl had been alternately sullen with jealousy or especially eager to please her husband. She continued to cook his meals and to supervise the tanning of the buffalo hides and to care for the lodge as before. In truth, Iron Nose decided, she gave him far more pleasure than the white woman.

She was the only white woman he had ever possessed in this way, and he wondered if all others of her people were the same. Perhaps that explained why the white man was so often wild and angry and unpredictable. How could a man be at peace within himself when he had neither peace nor pleasure in his lodge?

Iron Nose did not beat the drum and make public the fact that he had found the white captive wanting, that she was lazy and unskilled and cold in her heart, and he didn't want her any more. Had he done so, any other warrior in the village might have claimed her. Having captured the woman and publicly taken her as a wife, Iron Nose was reluctant to admit that he had received a poor trophy in return for his bravery in the battle with the wagons. Instead he turned the woman over to Standing Owl and her family. They would teach her at least to be useful and obedient. Perhaps in time she would even wish to regain his favor, beseeching him to receive her again in his bed. When she did, Iron Nose thought, he would laugh at her. In the meanwhile Standing Owl was restored to her rightful place in the first tipi.

For Jaine Bryant the change made her life among the Comanches more difficult but easier to endure. Standing Owl's jealousy, long obvious, had been held in check. Now that the captive was no longer in favor, and while Iron Nose was often away for days or weeks at a time on a hunting mission or war party, that jealous anger was vented fully and with great satisfaction. The captive was given the most menial tasks to perform. At every missed step or mistake Standing Owl, her sister Hopping Bird, and her mother, who was called Cut Ear, laughed and mocked and spat upon the white captive, or drove her with willow sticks to move faster and work harder, as one drove a mule or a dog. Even young children of the village, seeing this treatment, delighted in taking part, making a game of teasing the captive, sometimes even throwing stones at her, shrieking with laughter when one caused her to trip and spill a water bag or to drop an arm load of dry sticks gathered near the riverbank.

Under this humiliation, many of the Comanches thought, the slender white captive would surely break. Instead a slow change took place. She grew even thinner, all softness burned away by hard work under the relentless sun. She was not even welcome in the "squaw-cooler," or wicky, a kind of arbor made of leafy boughs laid across a crude pole frame elevated on four posts, which gave cool shelter for the other women during the hot spells of late summer. But she neither complained nor crumpled. She grew stronger. And with the physical change, which found her menial duties becoming easier with each passing day, there was an inner change. A numbness of spirit had settled over her when Iron Nose forcibly claimed her as a wife. Now she began to emerge from it. She was still *alive.* She would suffer whatever came to her, and survive. Somewhere Ter was also alive, searching for her, waiting for her to be found. Jaine had heard of captive women being bought back from the Indians. Some day it might happen to her. She had only to endure.

The Comanches, to whom courage was a way of life, stoicism a virtue, respected the change in the white woman. Even Iron Nose regarded her with less scorn, acknowledging that she had never really given herself to him, that her stubborn refusal to accept him was not coldness but silent resistance. That he could understand. It was a warrior's trait.

One day, without guile but on impulse, Jaine Bryant admired with her eyes and expressions of wonder an elaborately decorated cradle that Standing Owl had just finished making, for she was full with Iron Nose's child. After that Standing Owl relented. The squaws no longer taunted or beat the captive. Although she remained a slave, her lot became easier.

The days began to shorten. The first searching winds of autumn blew down from the north across the naked prairie. Jaine's immediate fears eased, her grief lying quiet within her, she began to observe the life of the village with new understanding. She watched the preparations for battle when Iron Nose was to lead another war party north—the beating of the drums, the dancing and chanting, the elaborate ceremonies, the donning of paint not in meaningless daubs, as she had thought, but according to careful ritual. It was all medicine, she realized. It was meant to strike fear into the hearts of the Comanches' enemies and to preserve their own warriors from harm in battle.

While the men were away from the village, life went on, family and tribal life. The white captive, who was now called Willow, enjoyed more freedom, but she was never left completely alone, never unwatched. In a way she was treated like a child in Iron Nose's family, for the children of the village were seldom alone. Brothers, sisters, cousins, aunts and uncles, grandparents and parents were always fussing over them. They were savages, Jaine Bryant reminded herself, but acts of kindness and affection were all around her. And love. Whatever atrocities the warriors might commit against their enemies, they never raised their hands to noisy or disobedient children.

The foray to the north went badly. Iron Nose's band returned with the bodies of dead and wounded. They had cut hair from the manes and tails of their horses in mourning. Not only had they failed to steal any new horses, they had lost many of their own.

The grieving in the village lasted for days. Newly widowed women slashed their arms and legs cruelly and cut their hair. Their keening sorrow could be heard day and night. A few squaws turned on Willow, spitting at her and driving her away. She was part of Iron Nose's lodge, but she remained a white woman. She learned that the war party had been badly mauled in a clash with bluecoats.

Late in the time of the Yellow Leaf Moon a band of Kiowas came to the village. They were called the Bad-hearts, but they were brothers to the Comanche, and they came in peace. That night, from a distance, Willow observed part of the pipe-smoking ceremony. The men, both Kiowas and Comanches, sat in a circle at the center of the village in front of the large council lodge. Jaine had previously been puzzled about the pipe. It was smoked not for pleasure, as men smoked in her experience in the white world, but in a ceremonial, almost religious way. The pipe itself was handsomely worked and decorated. Iron Nose's pipe, which she had examined closely in his tipi, had a red stone bowl and a smooth, painted wooden stem, decorated near the mouthpiece with a miniature beadwork shield from which hung several very small black-and-white feathers. As the pipe was passed around the circle of brothers, she realized that every movement, every word and reply, was ritualized, as precisely as a formal dance.

Thinking about it later in the darkness of the lodge, in which a low fire burned now because the nights were cold, she realized that she had found the ceremonial smoking of the pipe fascinating. Through it she had seemed to come closer to understanding the nature of her captors, and she found herself unable, that night, to summon up the hatred that had sustained her during her first weeks of captivity. She could still not look at Iron Nose without a feeling of revulsion crawling over her, but she could no longer summon up the fervor with which, every single night of that first month, she had prayed for his death.

During the next moon, the Moon of Early Frost, Iron Nose rode away at the head of a hunting party. He was the real leader of the village, although his uncle, Twisting Wind, the peace chief, was the oldest and wisest of their leaders, treated always with the utmost respect even though he no longer rode out to battle or to the hunt. Watching Iron Nose on his brown-and-white pony, Jaine thought of the harm and grief he had brought to her and Ter, to Mary Cadigan and others of the wagon caravan. To the Comanche the raid and the successful theft of horses and women had been acts of heroism rather than evil. They had won him honor. What was evil then, and honor?

Strange notions for a white slave, she thought.

But she had not come meekly to accept her situation. The women and children and old ones of the village paid less attention to her as time passed, accepting her as part of the village. She had been waiting for another time when the men would all be away. She was planning her escape.

It was not to be. Two days after departing on the hunt the men returned in great haste. A hurried council was called. As Jaine Bryant watched and wondered, aware of the excitement throughout the village, she saw the women gathering their children, horses, mules, and even many of their dogs around the tipis, securing the animals on ropes to keep them near.

The order came. The village must move. An attack was feared.

With the remarkable speed and efficiency Jaine had observed in one previous move to a different place along the river bottom, the tipis were taken down. Within a minute after Twisting Wind's lodge cover was seen flapping in the wind, having been loosened from the frame, all of the covers were similarly blowing and flapping. A moment later all of the covers had been removed. The lifting pole was freed, the anchor rope released, and suddenly all of the lodge poles were flat on the ground. Less than ten minutes from the time of Twisting Wind's signal, the entire village was on the move. Dogs and horses and mules were all used as beasts of burden, a balanced load of poles dragging from each side of some, others carrying packs of supplies or pulling a kind of dragging sled behind, called a travois. While most of these platforms carried household goods, tools and food, Jaine saw several children and at least one old woman riding on some of the larger, horse-drawn platforms.

The caravan thus formed seemed to assemble in a haphazard way, but it was soon clear that it could move at a very brisk pace. Throughout that day there was no halt. At times scouts raced out ahead of the column or ranged behind it. Jaine began to realize that the Comanches feared pursuit. Soldiers? She hardly dared to hope.

Would Iron Nose allow her to be recaptured? If it came to a fight, would he kill her rather than let her go?

She didn't know. She had begun to understand something of Indian ways, but she knew that she had hardly scratched the surface of her captor's mind. She knew now that Indians were not invariably or senselessly cruel, as she had believed before, in spite of the heartless savagery inflicted upon Mary Cadigan. They acted according to their own customs, their own ways, their own concepts of right and duty. Might those ways dictate that Iron Nose could not with honor let her be recaptured?

In late afternoon it was necessary to cross a stream. Here again the nomadic Indians revealed their efficiency. Tipi poles were taken from some of the horses and quickly tied together to form rough rafts, on which the travois and the other packed belongings were ferried across with little loss of time, most of the baggage still dry when reloaded on the far side of the river.

They moved on. As darkness gathered around them Jaine could hear the warriors, riding well ahead of the rest of the column, chanting their songs. The night was filled with the jingling of bells and barking of dogs excited over the move and the songs of the brave men of the tribe. She could almost feel part of it, she thought. She was Willow, and this was her village. How long had she lived among these people? She knew for certain only that it was late in the year, late fall or early winter. Although she had lost track of the days long ago, there had been several snow flurries recently, and the nights were very cold. She understood that the hunting party which had returned in such frantic haste had been sent to kill buffalo to supply the village with meat through the winter. Bitter weather was near. And it had been late July when she was captured. Three months ago at the least, perhaps longer.

Around midnight the caravan at last rested.

There was much talk around the small fires in the camp that night. While Jaine could speak only a few words in the Comanche tongue, she had come to understand a great deal of what she heard. She was able to piece together the story of the aborted hunt.

That was how she learned that the Comanches were fleeing not from white pony soldiers but from rival Indians, a war party larger and better armed than theirs, with many more rifles.

The hunters had quickly found a herd of buffalo on the open plain north of the canyon of the Canadian where the village had spent most of the summer. They had followed the buffalo in order to set up the most effective kill. When they had finally made their attack, they had unexpectedly encountered a group of Cheyennes, who had been trailing the same herd southward for several days. Rivalry flared into anger. Shots were exchanged. Seeing that the Cheyennes were outnumbered, Iron Nose and his warriors had struck at them in full force, killing or wounding many.

But some of the enemy had escaped. And they had carried word of the attack to a much larger Cheyenne village to which these hunters belonged. That village was less than a day's hard ride to the north. When Iron Nose's scouts reported that the Cheyennes were beating the drum and performing scalp dances, preparatory to setting out to claim vengeance against the Comanches, who were their traditional enemies, Iron Nose and his party had been forced to abandon the buffaloes they had been following and to retreat.

The flight of the village was not considered cowardly but prudent. To escape Cheyenne vengeance would be a kind of victory. And if the Cheyennes failed to catch them quickly, it was argued, their war cries would begin to lose some of their fervor, and they would begin to doubt their medicine. And the coming of the snow blanket to the prairie would effectively end pursuit.

Jaine Bryant slept fitfully, for she sensed that, with all their show of bravery and their very real courage in battle, the Comanches were nervous. The Cheyennes were also brave. They rode in great numbers under the protection of the magic arrows. They were led by a mighty chief of their tribe.

She thought again of trying to slip away from the camp during the night, but she knew that the horses were all picketed and closely guarded against any attempt by the enemy to steal them. She thought of the bleak wilderness through which she had walked that day with the rest of the moving village, and of the angry Cheyennes who were somewhere out there on the prairie, donning their war paint and chanting their war songs of courage and glory. And what if the great blizzard of which some of the Comanches had spoken caught her alone and on foot in the wilderness? What chance would she have to live through it?

The desire to escape was tempered by hard realities. She would wait, she told herself. For the moment she was safer traveling with the Comanches, who no longer seemed to intend her any harm as long as she stayed with them.

At last she slept. In the darkest hour before dawn she was still sleeping, and she did not hear the soft bird calls that seemed to come from all around the camp, bringing uneasiness to the sentries who were awake, listening.

When the first gray light streaked the earth line to the east and the Comanche camp was dimly visible in the early gloom, there was another call, melodious and insistent, from some distance away.

It was followed almost immediately by a shrill, ululating cry that could only have come from a human throat.

That scream brought Jaine Bryant to her feet, trembling, as the first whooping line of Cheyenne warriors materialized like ghosts out of the shadowy ground mists, hurling themselves on their ponies against the Comanche village.

7 / The White Comanche

ONE

The Cheyennes called themselves *Tsis-tsis-tas*, which simply meant that they thought of themselves as the "People," in much the same way as did the Apaches, the Comanches, and other Indian tribes. There were the People, and there were others. The *Tsis-tsis-tas* called the Comanches the "Snake Men."

The People had fought a great battle against the Snakes and the Bad-hearts at Wolf Creek nine summers before, at which Gray Thunder, the arrow keeper, was killed. The aftermath of that battle had been that peace had been declared between these ancient enemies. For seven winters there had been no war between the People and the Comanches.

In this year there had been much fighting on the plains, but it was warfare against the white invaders who killed the buffalo and destroyed the grass. The Kiowas, Apaches, and Comanches had asked the Cheyennes and Arapahoes to join them in alliance against their common enemy, but the People refused. They remained at peace. Their chiefs in council had declared that there would be no war songs, no beating of the drums, no hostile actions taken against either the white men or their brothers of the southern tribes.

But now a band of the Snake Men had attacked a smaller group of Cheyennes who were hunting the buffalo. Four out of seven young warriors on the hunt had been killed. Among them was Standing Crow, brother of Two Tails.

Two Tails was not a hot-blooded young warrior but a chief who had seen some forty summers. His face, like the earth's, was seamed and lined and crossed by many tracks. He had loved his brother. Now he had vowed to avenge Standing Crow's death.

It was a hard decision, for the council of the People had decreed that the tribes were at peace. If Two Tails kept his pledge to his brother, he was subject to punishment, even to the probability of banishment from the Cheynne council. He would become an outlaw, and his lodges would have to be raised apart from those of the People.

It was a hard decision but he did not hesitate. A vision came to him in the night, banishing all doubts. In the dream he looked down into a great sink, whose level floor was covered with the bodies of Snake Men. Only one figure stood erect in the basin, and the skin of that lone survivor was white. On top of the far rim overlooking the sink another solitary figure rode back and forth.

This one was clearly a warrior, for he carried his lance held high and he lifted his voice in his war song. Two Tails recognized the song. It was that of his brother, Standing Crow.

There were many young men among the People eager to fight, for it had been many winters since they had known the joy of riding out to battle. Among them were members of two of the Soldier societies, the Red Shields and the Crooked Lances, or *Him-ow-e-yuhk-is*. The Dog Soldiers, largest and most powerful of the Soldier societies, refused to follow Two Tails, remaining obedient to the council.

Two Tails went to Rock Forehead, keeper of the sacred arrows, with a horse and other gifts, asking that the medicine arrows be renewed. But Rock Forehead hesitated, making excuses. It was not the right time, he said. New feathers would have to be collected. The ceremony of renewal itself would take many days. It would be dangerous to go into battle without favorable influence from the arrows, which had supernatural powers. He counseled patience.

In anger Two Tails withdrew. He knew that Rock Forehead was reluctant to renew the arrows because of the council's decree. But he told his followers of the vision that had come to him in the night. It was all the medicine he needed, for Standing Crow would surely not have come to him in the dream if it were false.

The eager band of warriors separated from the village and began preparations for battle, singing war songs and painting their war horses. Among them was Spotted Dog, a young and very brave leader who would, along with Two Tails, carry the pipe against the Snakes. The war party, which numbered fifty-two braves, moved south into the dry lands where the Snake people roamed. Scouts were sent ahead to find the enemy.

The next day the scouts returned, exultant, for their success would earn them scouts' feathers. They had found the Snake Men. It was a large village, numbering many men and women and children, moving eastward. One scout had sneaked close to the village and identified Cheyenne ponies among their horses. One, he said, was the pony Standing Crow had ridden to the hunt.

Through the afternoon and evening after the return of the scouts the warriors prepared for the fight. They donned war paint and completed the painting of their war horses. They checked their equipment. They sang their war songs. A pile of buffalo chips, symbolizing the enemy, was placed at the center of their camp, and the mounted young men raced toward it, each trying to be the first to touch the chips with his lance, for three men were allowed to count coup in this way upon the "enemy."

Two Tails had decided upon a night march. The Snake village was large, and he had heard of the prowess of its old chief, a brave and mighty warrior named Twisting Wind, and of a younger leader known as Iron Nose. The Cheyennes would try to surprise them.

The night was cold and windy, with occasional light snow flurries blowing like white dust, but the wind was at the backs of the Cheyennes and this was seen as a good omen. The enemy had camped beside the twin ponds in the big bend of Beaver Creek, raising their temporary tipis on the flats north of the creek, which at this time of year, when the late false summer had ended, was mostly dry, with only small pools and trickles along the shallow bed. Two Tails decided to cross the Beaver some distance to the west. He would then circle back to attack the Comanches from the south across the creek, hoping that they would not expect an attack from that quarter.

When this approach had been made successfully, the enemy camp discovered without giving away their own presence, Two Tails and his war party drew up to wait for the first light. They were within sight of Beaver Creek and the Comanche camp less than a mile away. The warriors were eager now, excited by the prospect of battle, for this was an exhilarating time, a chance to win great honors denied them during the years of peace. It was all well and good for old warriors to smoke the pipe of peace, but many of these younger braves had never had the opportunity to ride into battle. It was their first time, and the soldiers had to watch them to keep the more eager ones from riding off prematurely and warning the enemy.

Impatiently they waited through the last hour of darkness. Two Tails thought of his dead brother, killed on the hunt when he had made no preparations for battle, or for death. He remembered his vision and knew that it was true. Many of the Snake Men would die this day.

As soon as there was enough light to see dimly, long before the sun rose above the earth line to look upon the new day, Two Tails and Spotted Dog mounted, the others following suit. This time they rode not their travel ponies but the war horses they had led until the battle was imminent. A few warriors were sent out to attack the camp from the east and west, so that the enemy would not be certain where he should concentrate his defenses. A small group of younger warriors, six in all, were given the assignment of driving off the Comanches' horses if possible, for the Snake Men were known to be skilled riders, their horses very swift, and if they succeeded in mounting their horses they might all escape.

The Cheyenne raiders rode out eagerly, unafraid, for what man wished to grow old in his tipi, and to walk crippled with a stick to aid him, when it was possible to die in the fierce glory of battle?

TWO

Iron Nose had been uneasy all night. He had posted sentries north and west and east of the camp, neglecting only the creek at his back, knowing that the enemy, if he came, would be riding from the north. Even before it was light Iron Nose was up, prowling the perimeter of the camp, making certain that the horses were all safe, sending out scouts to ensure that no attacking party could surprise them. As soon as it was possible to see without confusion, the women began to take down the night shelters and to bundle up the gear that had been unpacked for cooking.

The attack came without warning. One moment there was only a mist hanging over the creek bed and in the ground hollows, obscuring vision and adding to Iron Nose's uneasiness. Then, as if they had materialized out of the mist, mounted Cheyennes were charging across the creek, whooping and shrieking. They had found this south flank of the camp unwatched, undefended. The first wave splashed across the creek bed and swept into the camp unmolested, creating instant panic and confusion.

Jaine Bryant saw Iron Nose leap onto his horse, which he had nearby. Other warriors ran for their ponies. At the same time there was a sudden commotion at the east end of the camp, where the ponies had been picketed for the night. Dust and powdery snow from a light fall during the night billowed up amidst a flurry of hoofbeats. Many of the Comanches felt dismay as they realized their horses were being driven off.

The yelping of dogs and the screaming of frightened children added to the turmoil. The Cheyennes had bows and arrows and lances and rifles. First one wave and then another broke over the camp. As they raced through, some fired arrows or bullets, others touched the demoralized Snake people with their lances, counting coup. Although most of the Comanches were on foot, they fought bravely. One man went down, struck in the hip by a lead ball, but he sat up, firing his rifle from that position until one of the Cheyennes rode by and drove his lance deep into the wounded man's back. Some of the Comanche squaws tried to gather up their children and run for safety. Others seized rifles and fired at the invaders. Still others sought out pits and hollows that would offer some protection and prepared to fight from there.

Among the first to fall were Twisting Wind and his aging wife. When she was shot down and cried out in fear and pain, Twisting Wind, having almost reached safety himself, turned back to her. Spotted Dog counted coup on both the woman and the old chief. He also fired the bullet that felled Twisting Wind. Then other warriors shot arrows and lead balls into the two bodies until they lay still.

Iron Nose had rallied some of his young braves and made a stand at the west end of the camp, where many of the Snake Men took cover behind some low sand dunes, hastily throwing up breachworks of sand and firing over them. Iron Nose had lost his horse, but not his courage or his instinct for command.

Others of the Comanche village, including a number of women and children and old ones, had escaped across the creek after the waves of Cheyennes had all crossed it to invade the camp. They shot sporadically from cover.

Among a handful of women and children who had sought shelter in the brush near the creek at the east edge of the camp was Jaine Bryant.

By now Iron Nose was directing heavy fire from the bulwarks to the west, and many Cheyennes had been wounded or killed. Several horses had also fallen. Wishing to avoid heavier casualties, Two Tails tried to make his voice heard above the yelling and shooting and the screaming of wounded animals. He wanted to regroup his forces north of the camp, away from the heaviest fire of the Snake Men.

At about this time two events occurred that determined the further outcome of the battle.

One involved the white woman. A Cheyenne had discovered the nest of women and children in the brush. Crashing among them on his war horse, he drove many from cover. Other Cheyenne soldiers joined in the pursuit, for they made little distinction between men and women in battle. A warrior named Runs-With-A-Limp saw Jaine Bryant trying to escape toward the creek. He rode at her, counting coup with the tip of his lance. Although the spear point made only a slight nick in the flesh of her arm beneath the shoulder blade, because she was running the impact of that light blow was enough to spill her to the ground. Runs-With-A-Limp wheeled his horse about, intending to kill the fallen woman. She was sitting up, holding out one hand in a futile gesture at warding off the blow that was coming.

At this point Two Tails saw her. Her pale skin was instantly obvious, and suddenly the meaning of part of his vision was clear. The woman must survive or his vision would be untrue. Quickly Two Tails rode between Runs-With-A-Limp and the white Comanche. "No!" he shouted. "She is white—she must live!" His action caused the other warrior's horse to veer aside, and the woman was saved.

In her terror Jaine Bryant did not comprehend

the Cheyenne chief's action. She had a glimpse of his imposing figure astride a magnificent dun-colored horse. From his splendid headdress of eagle feathers she knew that he was a chief, and she knew that he had saved her life for some unknown reason of his own. A moment later he reappeared out of the dusty turmoil of the fighting, directing another Cheyenne brave on foot to lead a pony toward the white woman. Without a word the young warrior seized her and lifted her onto the pony's back. Then she was led away.

While this occurred, the second significant turning point in the fight took place. Iron Nose saw a riderless Cheyenne war horse pull up near his defenses. He ran to seize the horse's trailing single rope rein. Spotted Dog, who had already distinguished himself in the battle, saw Iron Nose in the open. He could not resist the chance to count coup on the leader of the Snake Men. Ignoring Two Tails's shouts to withdraw, Spotted Dog urged his horse into a run. As he galloped toward the Comanche chief, many of the other enemy warriors saw him and began to fire. Miraculously he rode through a shower of arrows and bullets unhurt. Then, as he drew back his lance while bearing down upon Iron Nose, a Cheyenne arrow caught him full in the face. The momentum of his charge carried him on, completing the hurl of his lance. As Spotted Dog fell sideways from his racing horse, his lance drove on, plunging deep into the chest of Iron Nose. The Comanche leader fell back, mortally wounded.

That was the end of the battle, except for a few last coups and meaningless shots. Two Tails saw that he had won a great victory, although the cost was high. Cheyenne bodies lay among the Comanche dead in the clearing where the enemy camp had been, a creek bottom that resembled the sink of his vision. It came to him that the rescue of the white Comanche alive, also part of his vision, was a signal, and that now was the time to withdraw.

The surviving remnants of the Comanche village escaped unmolested across the creek, where their swollen numbers now presented a formidable line of defense against further attack. Two Tails directed that all of the dead and wounded of his war party should be gathered. With them, along with several captured women and children, including the white woman, the Cheyennes moved away, assembling north of the battleground. Two Tails found that they had collected twenty-eight of the Snake people's horses, including six identified as having been stolen Cheyenne ponies.

In the battle the People had suffered three men killed, including Spotted Dog, and more than a dozen wounded. It was not known how many of the Comanches were dead, but their casualties were many times those of the Cheyennes. Both of their chiefs had fallen, and already the cries of their mourning women filled the air.

Less than two hours after the attack began, Two Tails led his war party away to the north. Their war songs, now songs of victory, drifted back over the bloodstained sand of the creek bottom.

Two Tails knew that his unsanctioned action would make him an outlaw among his own people, but his heart was full of joy. No longer would Standing Crow ride back and forth on the rim above the field of battle. Now he could go in peace on the journey that had no end. His death had been avenged.

THREE

Two Tails was allowed to claim no public honors for his victory over the Snake Men at Beaver Creek. Instead he and the warriors who had followed him were punished by being declared outlaws. They were banished from the council fires of the People.

Had it been otherwise, Two Tails would have brought the white Comanche captive into the main Cheyenne village on the Arkansas, not far from Bent's Fort. Even if the other chiefs had not deemed it wise to turn her over immediately to the white people at the fort, almost certainly she would have been seen by the wives of white men living in the village or by other whites who came that winter, including Tom Fitzpatrick, the new Indian Agent, or even by William Bent, whose Cheyenne wife kept her lodge in the village, where her husband joined her as often as his duties permitted.

But as it happened Two Tails said nothing of the white Comanche, nor was she seen by any white man. Gathering together his family, including his two wives, who were sisters, Two Tails led all of his followers north of the Arkansas to search for a winter camp. After several days journey they set up their lodges near the junction of Rush Creek and Big Sandy Creek.

The white Comanche, who was called by her Comanche name of Willow, was docile. Two Tails treated her kindly, holding her under his own protection, for the story of her part in his war vision was now well known.

Soon after the tipis were raised in the new location of Two Tails's village, the time of the White Moon came, when snows fell for days on end and there was no good hunting, and the great plains lay quiet under the deep snows.

Two Tails saw that the white captive was unhappy, but she was not foolish, and she made no effort to run away across the white, unmarked wilderness of the winter prairie.

She had lived in the village of Two Tails for the cycles of two full moons before the white man came to smoke the pipe with the Cheyenne chief.

FOUR

Angus Haws had spent nearly a month in the Valle de Taos, drinking and brooding. During most of that time he had lived with a Mexican woman, whom he had seized for a violent, thumping fandango during the New Year's celebrations in one of the taverns of the settlement. But she was dirty and quarrelsome, she carried as many gray-backs in her hair as any Indian squaw, and she would cook nothing but the spicy foods favored by the Mexicans.

Near the end of January, as he had intended all along, Haws left Taos to accompany a caravan heading for Bent's Fort. At the fort he did not linger for long, but continued downriver, visiting several of the clustered Cheyenne villages wintering near the fort or along the Arkansas or at Big Timbers. He came near buying a Cheyenne from an old man with many children, but she was already mature and she was fat and ugly. A year before these factors might not have deterred Haws, since he was not anxious to pay a high price and the woman's father was eager to make a bargain. But this time Haws scowled, finally shook his head, and moved on.

At Big Timbers he heard about the white Comanche who lived in the village of Two Tails.

The news seemed to fan a spark in Haws. His questions about the white Comanche yielded little information, but a fire burned now in his blood, a fire lit in the past summer by his chance glimpses of the emigrant woman at Bent's Fort. He had given little thought for many years to marrying a white woman. There were none to choose even if he wished, and in any event, like most mountain men, he preferred an easy liaison with an Indian squaw, obtained cheaply or for nothing, a woman hardworking and used to the wilderness life, which few white women would have found endurable.

But a white Comanche was different. She had lived among Indians. She knew their ways. She was not simply a toy to place on a shelf. It was possible, of course, that she was not white at all but a light-skinned Mexican. Or she might have been captured as a child, in which event, though light of skin, she would be as much an Indian as any woman Haws could choose.

He could not deny his interest. Learning the location of Two Tails's outlawed village, he headed north across the snow-covered prairie. It was hard going. At times he floundered through drifts that reached to his horse's belly, but Haws had no fear of the land or its elements. If another storm came up, he could dig down into a snow-bank and create a shelter in which to survive, or use, as Indians and animals did, the prairie's invisible natural shelters, a gully or canyon sheltered from the wind, a shoulder of rock to nest behind.

Haws brought with him the horse he rode, his three pack horses, and another Indian pony he had purchased with the little money he received for his fall take of beaver plews. As additional trade goods he also had beads, colored cloth, cooking pans, two flintlock rifles, and ammunition.

He found the village by following Big Sandy Creek to the fork where Rush Creek flowed into it. The distance was some thirty miles or so from the Arkansas in a straight line, more like fifty miles as Haws traveled it in the snow. The weather was clear and bright but bitter cold. The moisture from his breath froze in his beard. Snow glare made his eyes raw.

The smoke from Cheyenne fires guided him for the last two days, visible over long distances against the crystal clarity of the winter sky. During that time he traveled less than twenty miles.

Snowed in, keeping to their tipis during this Hard-Time Moon when the days were just beginning to lengthen, the hibernating members of the

Cheyenne village showed little surprise over the appearance out of the snowy wastes of a lone, bearded white man. Only the village dogs, who set up their familiar din, and many children, seemingly immune to the cold, reacted excitedly to the visit.

Haws rode straight to the largest, most impressive of the lodges near the center of the village. There he was welcomed gravely by Two Tails, impressive himself in his great winter buffalo robe. The Cheyenne chief invited Haws to share the hospitality of his tipi, for he had not failed to note the trapper's string of horses and the packs they carried.

The white woman—captive or wife, Haws didn't know—did not appear that first evening, and he did not inquire about her. A bargain with an Indian chief could not be rushed without offending his dignity.

The next day Haws spoke of his need for a wife and of his desire to find one of his own skin, although he took care also to praise the beauty and usefulness of Cheyenne women. Two Tails listened sympathetically. He understood the white man's wishes, for were not all men the same in many ways? He saw at once that the stranger had heard of the white captive he had taken from the village of the Snake Men, and that he had come to buy her, but he did not immediately offer to produce her. Instead, when the midday meal was prepared and served in the lodge, one of the women in attendance, who kept her head bent and was silent, as were the others, was the white Comanche.

Angus Haws did not stare at her, but his keen eyes missed nothing. He did not recognize her then, but he saw that she was indeed a white woman, although her skin was deeply tanned. She dressed like the other women and her hands were callused from hard work, but her hair was strikingly different, its color a burnished gold, the hair woven into two long braids. Haws felt a surge of desire that only his naturally stoic expression, as unreadable as an Indian's, and his thick tangle of beard enabled him to conceal.

Serious bargaining began later that day, after the men had rested. At its height the white woman, in response to some unseen signal, entered the lodge again and took her place with Two Tails's two wives at the south end, for the chief's place was always on the north side of the tipi. By this time Angus Haws had reluctantly offered one of his pack horses as well as the spare pony, the two rifles, trade beads and cloth in exchange for the white Comanche. Two Tails was quite pleased with the bargain, although he did not immediately agree.

Two Tails was a man of wisdom and understanding. Also he did not wish to be at war with the white men, especially since it was known that many new pony soldiers had marched along the Arkansas, arriving at the great fort during the time of the first deep snows. He had no wish to keep the white woman, who had shown that she was unhappy in his lodge. This white man desired her. Now she would be happy again among her own people, and Two Tails would have demonstrated his friendliness, as well as receiving many valuable presents.

At this point Angus Haws rose and went to his bags, which were now almost empty. He returned to his place, sitting cross-legged on a robe facing Two Tails. He was carrying a gallon jug of Bent's Fort rum, which had cost him twenty beaver pelts.

Haws uncorked the jug and held it out toward Two Tails. The Cheyenne shook his head. Haws drank deeply, gave a gusty sigh and wiped his mouth with the back of his hand. Again he offered the jug. This time Two Tails accepted it and took a great swallow, which caused his eyes to water and his throat to burn. The liquid raced through his body on the way to his belly like a river of fire. When Haws held out his hand, the chief returned the jug with reluctance.

He watched as the white man carefully corked the jug and placed it alongside the stack of beads and cloth, the two guns and ammunition, the cooking pans and the bridles of two horses.

Two Tails nodded.

FIVE

The next morning Angus Haws saddled two of his remaining three horses, redistributing his gear as best he could, most of it going on one of the remaining pack horses, since the woman would have to ride the other. When he was ready the white Comanche, who was called Willow, was brought to him. Two Tails, whose face was unnaturally dark and whose belly was churning from the effects of the fiery liquid in the jug, nevertheless emerged from his lodge to show his respect. He was not accustomed to drinking the white man's whiskey, and he was glad to retreat to his robes in the tipi when the stranger and his new wife rode away.

Haws did not turn south along the trail he had followed to the village. Instead he headed west along Rush Creek toward the distant mountains. At the first bend, when the Cheyenne village was cut off from view, the woman urged her horse forward in spite of the dragging snow until she was alongside Haws.

"Thank God," she said. "I don't know who you are, but . . ." Her lips trembled. "Thank God for you."

Haws grunted, saying nothing. He was puzzled, strangely excited. The more he saw of her, the more familiar she seemed, and the more she reminded him of the beauty of the woman who had so deeply affected him at Bent's Fort. She was different, certainly, leaner and tougher, like the willow she had been named after, but she had the same color hair, the same large gray eyes. Haws realized that he had never had a woman remotely like her.

"My name is Jaine Bryant," the woman said. "I was captured in an attack on our wagon train last summer. It seems like a long time ago. I thought I'd never . . ." Her eyes filled, and for a moment she couldn't speak. "Who are you?"

"Angus Haws."

"I'm grateful to you, Mr. Haws. You can't know how much. My husband will pay you back for everything you paid for me—I know it was a great deal. You'll be rewarded, that I can promise you."

Haws's blue eyes, narrowed against the snow glare, peered at her without expression. "I didn't buy ye fer anyone else," he said. "Ye're my wife now."

She stared at him, not comprehending. "You don't understand. I'm married. My husband is alive. He's looking for me, I know he is. I have to find him."

"Ye'll do what I say," Angus Haws told her. "The sooner ye l'arn that, the better it'll be. I didn't buy ye to turn ye over to any cotton-shirt dandy. I'm yer husband now."

He started to ride on, but her hot words stopped

him. "Can't you hear what I'm saying? I'm a married woman—you can't *buy* me like that. I belong to someone else. You'll take me back to Bent's Fort. He'll find me there, I know he will."

"I kin buy ye, and I did," Haws said. His voice rumbled now with impatience, but he was not angry. His reaction was tempered by his growing astonishment, for he was now beginning to believe that this was indeed the woman in the white dress and bonnet who had seemed so remotely beautiful, so unattainable. Some incredible chance had thrown her his way, and nothing would make him give her up, certainly nothing that she said. "Mebbe ye did belong to a white man oncet, but ye've belonged to a Comanche buck since then, and to a Cheyenne after that. Now it's my turn."

"What kind of man are you?" she cried. "I tell you my name is Jaine Bryant! If you don't—"

"Ye be Willow to me," Haws cut in harshly. "And ye've talked enough."

His knees tightened and his horse moved forward.

"I won't go with you!" the woman cried. "I wasn't bought by any Indian, and I won't be bought by you."

Haws looked back calmly, the ice-blue eyes glinting. "Ye'll go with me. One way or t'other, ye'll go."

Then he rode on, not looking back, and her horse began to follow him without urging. With rising horror she stared at his back, for the first time permitting her mind to accept the awful reality of what was happening to her.

She was once again a captive, as certainly as she had been when Iron Nose carried her away from her wagon so long ago. And the man who claimed her now was as savage and brutal and determined as any Indian.

He was not even worried about her running away. He knew that in this winter wilderness she could not get far before he caught up to her, and she would not long survive alone.

Helpless, sick at heart and filled with a crushing despair, Jaine Bryant rode behind him across the endless white sea of the plains, her horse at the center of the small procession, the pack horse trailing behind her. *I'll die,* she thought. *I'll die before I'll let another man touch me, and claim what belongs to Ter alone.*

But she knew that she would not die. Pain and grief did not kill, and the pulse of life beat too strongly in her. She had been through too much to fall into a swoon, like one of those half-forgotten beauties of Natchez.

And somewhere Ter still searched for her. Somewhere he remembered and prayed and hoped.

Which betrayal was worse, the betrayal of wooden submission to hands and body she despised, or the final betrayal of giving up all hope?

For the woman Jaine Bryant had become, at the end of her long ordeal of captivity among the Indians, there could be only one answer.

8 / The Indian Battalion

ONE

Lieutenant Colonel William Gilpin, at the head of two companies of dragoons forming the Indian Battalion, had reached Bent's Fort in mid-November. He informed Tom Fitzpatrick, the Indian Agent, that he carried orders to protect civilians against the depredations of warlike Indians, and that his authority included the conducting of punitive expeditions against the Southern Tribes who remained hostile, with an eye toward determining for the War Department whether the southern plains could be pacified by such a mobile force of cavalry at large in the territory, or whether it would be necessary to build and occupy a series of forts at strategic points along the main-traveled routes to the West.

With their areas of authority overlapping, Fitzpatrick and Gilpin were soon at odds. Not long after his arrival the colonel moved up the Arkansas to Pueblo, where he set up his winter quarters.

The winter passed without event. Gilpin conferred regularly with such mountain men as came to the adobe fortress Jim Beckwourth had established on a bluff overlooking the Arkansas, at the foot of the Rockies. He learned that the Utes, Apaches, Pawnees, Comanches, and Kiowas were still engaged in hostilities, curtailed only by the elements, which also stopped the flow of travelers across the plains. During the summer and fall of 1847 these bands of hostiles were credited with having destroyed 330 wagons and killing 47 Americans. It was too much to allow to continue.

Accordingly Gilpin began preparations for what would be come known as the Winter Campaign of 1848 against the Southern Tribes, although the actual campaigning continued through the spring and well into summer.

Among the volunteer scouts and hunters who were signed up in the first week of March for the expedition were Tom Brock and Ter Bryant.

TWO

"He got too much bile in de blood," Long Tom Brock solemnly asserted.

Ter Bryant smiled. "Maybe. He's a good commander though, even if he does set himself high up on the scales."

The leader of the Indian Battalion, Lieutenant Colonel Gilpin, had been two years in the field.

He had accompanied General Kearny in the long and fateful march to Sante Fe in the summer of 1846, and on to California. He had participated in that winter's campaign against the Navajos. Then he'd fought his way with Doniphan across Northern Mexico in the spring. Hardly had he returned to Missouri before he received new orders to march two companies of the new Indian Battalion to Bent's Fort. It was now May of 1848, and Gilpin had been marching and fighting across the prairies for all of two years with little rest. No wonder he was irascible and short-tempered, Ter Bryant thought. And if he and his dragoons displayed hair-triggers when they came across any body of Indians, without taking much care to determine whether or not they were hostile, well, they had been shot at enough to explain if not always to justify their actions.

And the fact remained that the Indians all along the Canadian and the Cimarron, ranging north all the way to the Arkansas, were all too ready to fight.

But not always ready to clash head-on with the now battle-seasoned bluecoats. Lately the Indians had taken to waiting for Gilpin's battalion to go by, after which they would sneak in along his back trail and look for any caravans attempting to cross the plains. Gilpin had sent the two scouts back along his trail for just that reason.

"You think de colonel be right this time, *mon ami*?" Brock asked.

The question was revealing. It said that, in less than a year on the plains, Bryant had earned the experienced scout's respect for his cool judgment. Bryant might still defer to Brock's greater knowledge of the Indian tribes and the territory much of the time, but he had learned fast and he didn't forget what he'd learned when he was in the middle of battle smoke.

"I wouldn't be surprised. Pawnees hit those wagons out of Fort Smith only two days after we saw 'em go by. I doubt it was coincidence."

The two men rode slowly, partly to avoid raising dust and partly because a rapidly moving object was easier to see in the vastness of this mesquite prairie between the two forks of the Canadian. For the same reason they avoided riding along the high ridge between the two rivers where they might be skylined, keeping instead to the level plain and occasional washes, going up cautiously every once in a while to scan the terrain to the west, for there would be no immediate danger eastward where the battalion's dust rose thick above the prairie. The scouts ranged well south of the plain trail left by the dragoons, searching for sign of fresh tracks made by unshod Indian ponies.

For Ter Bryant the search was always two-pronged. He had done his job scouting for the dragoons, usually working in tandem with Tom Brock, but it was his personal quest that had brought him to Gilpin's battalion as a volunteer. Gilpin's expedition was designed to scour all of the hostile lands south of the Arkansas to the Canadian and even beyond, ferreting out every belligerent band of Indians. One of those might be the village in which Jaine was held captive.

Bryant would not believe that she was dead. He would never give up the search while any hope remained.

"Hold on, lad," Tom Brock said softly.

Bryant reined in. His gaze quickly followed the direction of his friend's. What he saw was no more than a faint haze of dust beyond a rim to the southwest, hardly more than the dust a light breeze might stir up. But it was more than that. Brock didn't make such mistakes.

They worked their way slowly toward the rim. They left their horses in a hollow and climbed on foot, wriggling over the last yards on their bellies. They raised their heads slowly just enough above the rim to bring a long, flat table into view.

Below them, fed by a shallow tributary creek that ran northeast toward Wolf Creek, was a dense tangle of shrublike plum trees mixed with a scattering of prickly pear. Through this low wood, which was perhaps fifty yards across, a trail twisted its way from north to south. From the level of the table itself the trail would surely have been invisible, and the single column of warriors, clad only in breechclouts or leggings, naked from the waist up except for a few head feathers and other ornaments, would have been effectively screened by the thicket of trees.

The column was riding south toward the Canadian River.

"By gar, damme if we ain't flushed us out some Comanche," Tom Brock said.

"Comanches? You sure?"

"Do I got to say everythin' twice, lad? Them's Comanch'."

The scouts watched in silence until the head of the column cleared the plum wood. There were about forty in the party, and they were wearing paint.

"They comin' or goin', Tom? Which do you think?"

Never hasty in answering an important question, Tom Brock squinted thoughtfully after the Indians. "It be this child's opinion they's comin'. No sign they's stole anythin' or taken any scalps, and I ain't seed none of 'em hurtin'. Yessiree, I'd guess they's comin'."

"That means their village is back a ways." Bryant gazed north.

"It be likely. We's got to tell the colonel right quick." Brock knew what was in Bryant's mind, and his reply was his way of saying that a search for the village would have to wait.

"You can do that, Tom. That village can't be far, and with the men away I could get a good look at it."

"If you didn't git yourself shot by a squaw," Tom Brock said reasonably, "you still couldn't make yourself understood, lad. Wouldn't do you no good to go there alone. Might be best if you hightailed it after de colonel. This child'll stay here and git some rest, and see them Comanches keeps goin' in the same direction."

There was no time to argue it, and besides Ter Bryant knew that Tom was right. After a moment's hesitation he scuttled back down to his horse. He set off eastward at a brisk trot for the first quarter-mile. Then he let his black out into a full run. The horse, which he had purchased from William Bent after his nearly disastrous desert crossing, was fresh and eager to run.

Ten minutes later he was in sight of the slow-moving battalion. It pulled up as someone saw Bryant's dust boiling up behind the column. Bryant galloped straight to the head of the formation, where Lieutenant Colonel Gilpin swung out to meet him. The scout skidded to a halt a few feet from the officer.

"Comanches, Colonel," he reported. "Heading south toward that wagon trail below the Canadian, it looks like."

"How many, Mr. Bryant?"

"We counted about forty, sir. Lookin' for trouble, from the paint they're wearing."

"Well, that's what they're going to find, Mr. Bryant," Gilpin answered crisply. He turned in the saddle. "Sergeant Cooper! Column about!"

A half hour from the time Bryant had left Tom Brock alone on the rim, the battalion commander was looking down at the plum wood and Brock was pointing out a shortcut to the south that would intersect the Indians' trail. Gilpin divided the battalion as soon as they reached the lower table, leading one company himself along the trail left by the Comanche ponies and sending another company in a flanking movement to the east. It would ride parallel with Gilpin's force, keeping well out of sight. It would close in fast only if it heard shooting or received word, thus hopefully catching the Comanches in a vise.

To his disappointment Ter Bryant was sent with the flanking column, while Tom Brock scouted ahead of the command force along with Sergeant Reeves, an enlisted scout who had been with Gilpin on the long march of the Army of the West.

For an hour the flanking company, led by young Lieutenant Sanderson, scrupulously obeyed Gilpin's orders to stay out of sight. During that time the only evidence they saw of anything alive in the desolate, fissured terrain north of the

Canadian was the dust of Gilpin's dragoons, and at times even that sign disappeared. Once Bryant had to ride out ahead to make certain that Gilpin hadn't altered course. Sanderson's dragoons trailed behind the others at a slower pace, trying not to send up as much telltale dust.

It was early afternoon when Bryant heard the distant crackle of rifle fire. Sanderson heard it in the same instant. It was impossible to estimate how distant the shooting was, for such sounds carried far. Sanderson's face lit up. He wheeled the column and they set off across an undulating plain toward a curving line of low brown hills to the southwest.

The Comanches, who had detected Gilpin's bluecoats in pursuit, had chosen not to run. True to the belligerence of the tribes across those southern plains that year, they attempted to ambush the dragoons, luring them along a trail that led into a valley between two smoothly rounded hills.

The Indian force was larger than reported—as Gilpin would angrily point out later to his civilian scouts—for some twenty or more Comanches had apparently passed ahead of the column spotted by Tom Brock and Bryant. The Comanches had split this force, hiding behind the brows of the facing hills.

Such a textbook tactic was not calculated to catch the experienced commander of the Indian

Battalion by surprise. After pretending to ride straight for the depression between the hills, at the last moment he swung his column and charged with his entire company up the western slope.

They rode through an initially heavy volley of arrows and bullets. Reaching the crest of the hill in that first furious charge, the bluecoats broke the back of the outmanned line of Comanches.

While the fighting continued heavy on this hill, the second group of about thirty Indians attacked on horseback from the eastward rise. To do so they had to cross the valley between the hills. Gilpin turned some of his dragoons to pin this attacking force in the hollow. The Comanches were caught there when Bryant came into view of the fighting, charging with Sanderson and the second company of dragoons at full gallop.

Most of the surviving Comanches fled. After a short run Gilpin called off the pursuit. His overriding purpose in this battle, as in others throughout the campaign, was not to kill as many savages as he could but to put the fear of God— and of the bluecoats—into the warring tribes, giving them warning and intimidating them into abandoning their hostilities. Even so, there were twelve Comanches dead at the end of the brief battle and five sullen captives, two of them wounded so badly that they had been unable to escape.

From the captives Tom Brock could not learn the location of their village, but he suggested to the colonel that it was almost certainly to the north and could be found by following the fresh trail. He surmised that the Comanches had probably left the village early that morning, for their horses had been fresh when first seen in the plum wood.

"Very good, Mr. Brock. Those who escaped will probably head for home as soon as they catch their breath. Let's see if we can't be there to welcome them!"

THREE

The Indian Battalion reached the Comanche village at dusk. It was half empty, inhabited only by women who would not leave their children or by old ones unable to flee. It was obvious that other squaws and children were hiding in the brush and ravines nearby. There was no sign of the presence of young warriors.

Gilpin and the battalion camped openly beside the village that night. He gave orders that no action should be taken against the hapless villagers. No one in the command should fire unless fired upon.

His display of "peace" did not go unnoticed. In the morning a dozen warriors rode in, claiming to have been away on a buffalo hunt. By midday most of the stragglers from the immediately surrounding plain had come back to their lodges, but the main body of younger braves stayed away.

Through Tom Brock, who spoke a surprising variety of Indian dialects including the Comanche, Gilpin spoke sternly of the White Father's desire for peace with the Comanches, and of the determination of his people to punish those who made war upon the wagon trains and other peaceful expeditions across the plains.

When this formality was over, Brock and Bryant went slowly through the village, questioning a number of women and old men. It was a ritual they had followed in a score of similar Indian camps and villages throughout the campaign, and in others before that. With each disappointment Bryant found the faith he clung to hammered thinner. Each blank face or indifferent shrug dealt a blow against his hope.

But this time Tom Brock found an old man, toothless and garrulous, who answered his questions at length. Brock's own expression remained unreadable as the talk went on. Bryant turned away, his heart pounding in spite of his resolve not to expect too much. When he looked back, Tom Brock was solemnly offering the old Indian a plug of his tobacco.

Brock looked at his friend. "He's told me

about a great victory a Comanche chief won last summer up near de headwaters of de Purgatoire. This chief stole many horses from de white-eyes."

"Anything else?"

"He say they also taken a woman captive."

Bryant's mouth was dry. "Only one woman?"

"That don't cut," Brock answered. "Might be they wouldn't have bragged about de one they killed, or no one would've remembered her very long. But this old one, he hear about de white woman who was taken. They no kill her."

Ter Bryant's tightly held emotion found release in a slow clamping and unclamping of his fists. He could no longer deny the hope. "It must have been Jaine. It had to be her."

"It seem likely, lad."

"Who was this chief? Does he know? Where is his village?"

The black man regarded him gravely. "His name was Iron Nose. He was a great chief of de Comanches, this one say."

"Was?"

"He run into some trouble with de Cheyennes. Dog me if I can figger out jist when it was. They doesn't remember things de way we do, lad, but it sound like it was early winter."

"My God, Tom, what happened?"

"Them Cheyennes, they attack de Comanches' village. Iron Nose was killed. *Beaucoup*

Comanches was killed. *Beaucoup* dead, that's all the old one can say."

"What about Jaine?" A band of pressure tightened around Bryant's skull as his anxiety increased. "Does he know what happened to the white woman?"

Tom Brock shook his head slowly. "He no can say if she be killed or taken captive again. But de Comanches from that village, they come by this one, beggin' for food in de winter. De white woman wasn't with them."

Bryant stared at him, then at the old man, whose seamed face was calm with the impassiveness of age. The old man spoke in response to the glance, his words meaningless. Bryant turned away, choking back a senseless rage that made him want to strike out at any Comanche, however old, however innocent.

"It don't mean she's gone," Tom Brock said quietly. "Don't mean that at all, dog me if it do. Listen to this child, lad. De Cheyennes, they could've taken her. They's at peace with de white man. She be safe with them. You think on that."

Ter Bryant nodded dumbly. There was still hope. He thought of all the months Jaine had been a Comanche captive, enduring hardship and punishment he could hardly imagine, only to be caught up in tribal warfare and carried off to still another unknown fate.

Or left behind unnoticed. Neither the surviving

Comanches nor the Cheyennes would have cared about one white victim of their fighting.

Angrily he shook off that bleak vision, refusing to accept its possibility. There was a chance that she was alive. She could be with friendly Indians. She might even now be waiting for him in the safety of Bent's Fort or a Cheyenne camp on the Arkansas. All he knew for certain was that his search was not over. It was only taking a new direction.

This occurred in the last week of May. It was the first word of any kind Ter Bryant had had of Jaine in ten months.

FOUR

In late August the tribes began to gather at Big Timbers, some forty miles downriver from Bent's Fort, where they awaited the return from Washington of the Indian Agent, Tom Fitzpatrick, who would bring presents and new talk of peace. From the Great Council of that fall of 1848 at Big Timbers would come Fitzpatrick's impossible dream of a conclave of all the tribes west of the Mississippi and a new era of harmony between red man and white.

Lieutenant Colonel William Gilpin of the Indian Battalion foresaw the future more accurately when he sent his adjutant general a gloomy assessment of his punitive expedition south of the Arkansas. "We have killed two hundred and fifty Pawnees, Comanches, Prairie Apaches, and Osages," he reported in August. But he confessed that there existed neither the troops nor the fortifications to control "this numerous cloud of savages." Continued warfare, he believed, was inevitable.

For the first time, however, there were Kiowas, Comanches, and Prairie Apaches represented in the huge gathering of Indians at Big Timbers, joining the more peaceful Southern Cheyennes and Arapahoes.

For weeks Tom Brock and Ter Bryant moved among the arriving villages, asking questions, sifting rumors. And at last, early in September, they found Standing Owl, the widow of Iron Nose of the Comanches.

Leaderless, decimated by prolonged warfare, the lodges of Iron Nose's people were empty of buffalo. Hunger as well as fear of Gilpin's battalion had brought them to the Council.

Standing Owl remembered the white captive. After receiving presents, she proved willing to talk about her. With some satisfaction she revealed that the woman had been captured by a great chief of the Cheyennes. She even knew his name: Two Tails.

The searchers soon discovered that Two Tails was not among the chiefs in the Cheyenne council at Big Timbers, for he was still an outlaw. But he was well known among the People, and although he had remained aloof from the gathering of the tribes, his village was only a short journey to the north.

Without delay Bryant and Brock rode north. Three days later they came to the isolated village of the outlawed chief, who received them in peace and friendliness. He spoke willingly of the white Comanche who had slept in his lodge, whom he called Willow. She had been unhappy, he said. She was like the two eagles who were kept in the cage over the entrance to the white man's great fort on the Arkansas, for she longed to be free among her own people. Then a white man had come across the snows of the plains during the Hard-Time Moon, bearing horses and gifts. Two Tails had known what it was good to do.

The white Comanche had been sold to the bearded Man-Who-Kills-Beaver, who had ridden away to the west—toward the mountains.

There was no question in Ter Bryant's mind that the woman called Willow was his wife.

FIVE

After leaving the village of Two Tails, Bryant and his companion rode directly to Bent's Fort, where their enquiries about a white trapper who had purchased a white woman proved fruitless. They continued upriver toward El Pueblo. With Gilpin's dragoons no longer quartered there, the small fort had once again become a hangout for idlers, gamblers, and free trappers. Someone there might have heard, in the mysterious way news traveled in the wilderness, about the trapper and a white woman.

Ter Bryant suffered every delay with ill-concealed impatience. The emotion that pushed him now was no longer the grief and guilt he had known for more than a year of agonizing search across the southern plains. He rode now with a smoldering rage. When they camped above the Arkansas, still a day's ride from Pueblo, he sat staring into their small campfire without thought of fatigue or needed rest.

"What kind of man would do such a thing?" he demanded of Tom Brock, not for the first time. "What kind of man would steal another man's wife?"

"I reckon he don't see it that way."

"What other way is there?"

"Some of de free trappers, they sees things different. He bought himself a woman, that's all he know. If he be like most, he bring her into Bent's Fort for sure. But some of de mountain men, they been livin' free too many year to take account of any law but what they want."

"He'll answer to me."

"Reckon he will. He won't give her up easy, lad, whoever he be. Man like that, he figger he pay for her, that's all. He no give her up, by gar."

Ter Bryant heard the comment with angry satisfaction. He didn't shrink from the prospect of a fight. In his mind was the conviction that a white man who would take another's wife by force—and he could not believe Jaine would have gone with him willingly—was worse than any red savage.

"I'll find them," he said harshly. "I'll find them, and he'll answer. You hear me, Tom—he'll answer."

The following day they arrived at El Pueblo. They were there when Henry Stallworth, a free trapper, crawled out of the foothills, more dead than alive, and collapsed at the fort's gates.

9 / Willow's Escape

ONE

She had become Angus Haws's woman. He had paid for her, she belonged to him, she would do his bidding. In the beginning, when all this had become clear, Jaine Bryant hated Haws with a bitterness at least as virulent as the anger she had felt toward Iron Nose. She opposed Haws in everything, forcing him to drive her at times with indifferent blows, as he would have whipped a stubborn mule.

Deep snows stopped their progress before they could travel far into the mountains. Haws found an abandoned trapper's shack which he shored up and covered with hides to keep out the worst winds and snowstorms. Here they waited out the killing cold of February and March.

Chilled and weakened by the ride across the snowbound plains and the punishing struggle into the foothills, Jaine Bryant went into a long, fever-ridden period of illness. When she began to pull out of it, regaining strength and the full possession of her senses, it was spring.

In the days that followed she slowly realized

that Angus Haws had nursed her through her illness.

They spoke little, for Haws was busy trapping beaver with the easing of the weather, and when he was with her in the crude shelter he was not talkative. He made no demands upon her, but he made sure that the fire in the mud fireplace would last during the periods when he was gone, he fed her meat broths that required some trouble in the preparation, he saw that she was kept warm and fed and safe.

By his own lights, Jaine thought, he cared for her as well as he could. At times, now that he was no longer compelled to punish her to compel obedience, he seemed almost gentle. More than once she caught him staring at her in an odd way, as if he were perplexed with himself.

In truth Angus Haws could not shake a sense of wonder over the fact that the woman of the caravan he had seen at Bent's Fort was now his woman, his wife. Although astonishingly changed by her long captivity, and more recently by sickness, she retained the fragile beauty that had kept her vision alive in his mind. She still moved him as no other woman had, touching emotions that had lain fallow since his childhood, and he could not help marveling at the capricious sequence of events that had thrown her his way.

In April, when she was once more on her feet, capable of light work to clean the shack and prepare meals, which she did out of a sense of obligation for the care he had taken to keep her alive, she tried to talk to him of her past life, hoping that his recent treatment suggested the existence of humane, decent impulses in the man.

"I'm grateful to you, Mr. Haws," she said, "for rescuing me from the Indians. I'm grateful for all you've done. But can't you understand that my husband must be searching for me? You know my name, you must have heard—"

"Ye be Willow to me," Haws answered bluntly. "That's all I need to know. Ye're mine now, and make no mistake about it."

That night, on her bed of boughs, he asserted his claim. Still weak, she was no match for him. Her resistance collapsed after a short struggle. Haws seemed not even to notice that she had tried to deny him. He took what he wanted with quick, brutal lust.

Soon after that they left the shack and moved higher into the mountains. Beaver had proved scarce in the foothill streams. Angus Haws continued to act as if the beaver would "come back," but in moving into the mountains he knew so well he was also retreating farther from civilization, strengthening his hold over the woman he had found.

The traveling was hard in melting snows and across swollen streams, but Haws forced their way with tireless energy and purpose. He knew

213

exactly where he was going, to the secret valley he had left in December, rich in beaver, a natural kingdom hidden from the world.

They entered it through the narrow pass from the north. With his return to the valley Haws felt a lifting of his spirits, a feeling of release, as near to joy as he was capable of feeling.

He had decided against building a cabin or makeshift shelter that might be seen and recognized as such by a chance wanderer. After several days he found what he sought, a cave high above the valley floor, screened by the tops of the tall pines that grew from the slopes below, inaccessible except on foot. The horses could safely graze in the meadows below, some distance from the cave.

Set into the valley's west wall, the cave was warmed by the morning sun, and free of prevailing winds. A hollow on the shelf at the cave's entrance shed smokeless warmth within and made a good place for a cooking fire. Layers of hides over pine boughs created comfortable beds inside. For Haws and his woman, Willow, this would be home.

In the isolation of the valley a different relationship slowly developed between them. Jaine had come to recognize the futility of physically resisting him. Moreover, she was in awe of the high wilderness, of the forest animals, including huge bears, of the incredible peaks and chasms and roaring rapids. Often when Haws was away, setting out his traps in the evening or going in the mornings to find his pelts, or when he was hunting game, she was frightened over being alone. In spite of herself she had to acknowledge her dependence on him.

Out of necessity—and perhaps because of something in her character that she could not deny—she shared more and more of his life. She had learned many things while living with the Comanches, including how to flesh and treat a hide. From Haws she soon learned how to "grain" his pelts and stretch them over the willow withes to dry. She did all of the cooking now, gathered wood for the fire, kept the cave clean. On the nights when he claimed her, she did not resist, and Haws did not notice, afterwards, her silent tears.

As she came to understand this solitary, angry man better, she could not hate him completely. Haws misunderstood this and the other changes in her. He began to believe that she had accepted her lot with him, in the way of any of his Indian women. But she was lovelier than any of them, quieter and gentler. When she was moved by something, a spray of flowers in the meadow near the lake, the sight of a young deer flitting through the pine forest, or the call of a bird, she was capable of a sweet delight that stirred strange emotions in a man who had known only harshness in his own life and, in women, passions and manners as wild and rough as his own.

When Haws knew that it was time to try to sell his take of beaver plews, for he was now in need of supplies, he felt a new reluctance to return to the places where he was known, such as Taos and Pueblo and Bent's Fort. He had no real fear of encountering Willow's husband, if indeed the man had not abandoned any search for her. But the thought of such a chance meeting—and more particularly of discovery, the revelation that he had bought a white woman from the Cheyennes and kept her for himself forcibly—made him uneasy, awakening an instinctive sense of danger.

He thought of going northwest to the fort Jim Bridger had established on the Black Fork of the Green River a few years ago. Haws had known Bridger in the old days—young Jim then, only a few years Haws's senior—and Jim would surely pay as well for plews as any Taos trader or Bent's people. It might be that he'd pay more, for Bridger knew the true value of fine pelts.

But that was a long haul over the mountains. Would he take Willow with him? He wouldn't dare have her come to Bridger's fort in his company, for that would start talk that would spread across the mountains and the plains. But could he safely leave her for the time it would require to make that long trek north?

Haws made a decision. Willow would have

to stay behind. Even if she tried to escape, she would find her way out of the valley only with great difficulty, and after that she would more readily become lost than follow tracks out of the wilderness. It was a risk to leave her alone, even for a short period, but he had seen Willow's fright of the mountains. He decided that she would be too afraid to face them alone. She would be safe enough in the cave, and for a time at least her fear would keep her there. And Haws meant to travel fast.

So it had to be Taos again. It was the closest place where he could sell or trade his plews.

He warned Willow against trying to leave the valley, or even straying far from the cave. He pointed out, truthfully enough, that the cave was out of the way of grizzlies. Once she came down, or attempted to leave the area, she would have to reckon with the great bears and all of the other real dangers of forest and mountain. Except for her skinning knife, she would be unarmed, helpless to defend herself. Her only safety was the cave.

Haws left in the first week of July.

For two days Jaine Bryant did nothing. This was the chance she had hoped for, but the fears Haws had cited were genuine. And she waited until she was certain that he had left the valley, guessing that he might wait to see if she would try to run away.

That second night, lying alone in the cave, she thought of Ter, of their first shining love, of their dreams and hopes. She needed those memories as an armor against panic. She knew that this had to be the time. She might not get another chance.

At dawn on the third day after Haws's departure, carrying a packet of meat and her skinning knife, she came down from the cave and set off on foot. Every sound, every shadow in the woods made her heart leap, but after a while these false fears eased. Most animals were more frightened of humans than they were of the animals—all except the grizzly. There was no sign of one of the big bears.

She had thought her sense of direction good, and she had the sun to guide her in a clear sky. The pass was to the north, she knew. It should be easy enough to find.

By midafternoon her panic was returning. She was still in the valley. One apparent trail had led her into an impassable canyon, another to a wide chasm she couldn't cross. The real pass seemed to have vanished.

She thought longingly of the cave. Warmth and safety. Snow still filled the shadowed crevices in the high walls and slopes above the timberline. In the open the night would be bitter. She would need to build a fire for warmth—and to keep night animals away.

The thought of eyes staring at her from the

darkness surrounding a fading campfire almost sent her back to the cave. A stubborn resolve drove her on.

She stumbled onto the north pass by chance, or plain persistence. Sooner or later she would have found it, although the opening was not visible from the floor of the valley, for the trail twisted back and forth and its canyon walls closed in first one way, then another, like a series of doors. Much of it was a narrow track and she scanned the way ahead anxiously. She didn't want to meet any bear lumbering toward her.

When she reached the top of the pass, the whole of the Rocky Mountains seemed to open out before her. She stared at the vista, splendid and intimidating, that stretched hundreds of miles to the north, east, and west, layer upon layer of soaring white peaks and dark green forests. How could she ever hope to find her way through such a wilderness?

Something caught her eye. She squinted hard. There it was, far off to the northeast, a thread of smoke wriggling upward until it vanished into the bright blue sky.

Smoke. Smoke meant a campfire. Angus Haws's fire? No, she was certain that he'd intended to swing south toward one of the forts or settlements where he customarily traded his pelts. Who, then? Other trappers?

Indians?

Behind her lay the valley and a life of enforced captivity as the woman of a man she didn't love and often despised. Ahead were unknown hazards, perhaps more terrible.

But she had to risk it.

She was hardly aware that the young woman who had started west a year ago with her husband could not have made the choice she made now. That woman—that girl, really—would have crouched miserably in her cave, shivering, escape only a dream of rescue.

But the woman standing at the crest of the pass knew that Ter would never find her there. She had to do it herself. She had to go on, no matter what came.

TWO

That night was one of unimaginable terror. It was the first time Jaine Bryant had ever been truly, completely alone in the wilderness.

With great difficulty she had managed to start a fire before dark, building it on a raised ledge both for safety and in the hope that her fire might be seen by friendly eyes. Resolutely she refused to accept the possibility that the builders of that other, distant fire might offer more of a threat to her than the wilderness itself.

She was unable to sleep. The pine forest in

which she found herself was filled with sounds and moving shadows. Twigs snapped under real or imaginary footsteps. The wind whispered incessantly. Branches swayed and rustled. Her fire seemed to catch the gleam of eyes watching her. The pale slopes of the high peaks seemed themselves to loom over her threateningly, and the vast reaches of land and midnight sky dwarfed her, shrinking her daring gamble to the feeble scratchings of the tiny, desperate creature she was.

She dozed fitfully and woke, trembling. Her fire was almost out. Hastily she threw more wood onto the pyramid. New flames leaped and crackled.

She thought of what this past terrible year must have been for Ter. How bitterly he would have blamed himself! The possibility that he might have given her up for dead long ago, that he might have gone on to a new life somewhere, haunted her. She hugged herself in her buffalo robe, shivering as much from the fear she had dredged up again as from the thin cold air or the unseen menace in the dark woods. He wouldn't have given up, she told herself over and over, like a litany. He wouldn't give up, and you can't.

As soon as it was light enough to see the path before her without stumbling, she was up and moving. She could no longer find the smoke that had caught her eye the day before. She could only trust her sense of direction to keep her moving toward the location of that fire.

But in the grassy meadows and wooded slopes of the mountains she was soon lost. Here there were no clear paths to follow. There were innumerable animal tracks that tempted her this way and that. She found and followed a water-course that led her between two forbidding peaks to another open park. She started across it. She was in the middle when she saw the grizzly.

It saw her in the same moment and stared with apparent curiosity. It was enormous when it stood erect on its hind legs. Jaine veered away from the bear, her heart thudding.

The grizzly started across the open meadow toward her.

She didn't know whether to run or keep walking steadily. The bear ambled after her, unhurried. If she ran, would that make the creature charge?

Fear decided her. She broke into a run toward the nearest trees. A glance over her shoulder showed the bear coming on steadily. In her panic she dropped her packet of jerked meat near the edge of a wooded slope. Stopping to retrieve it, she saw the bear much closer now, lumbering more quickly toward her. She abandoned the meat and fled.

Branches raked her arms and face as she blundered through the pines. The slope was steep and her legs soon ached. The blood pounded in her ears. She slipped on pine needles and fell. Scrambling up, she dared another look back. She caught a glimpse of gray at the edge of the trees and plunged on.

Now she no longer looked back. She had lost all sense of direction or purpose other than getting away from the huge bear. Floundering blindly up the uneven slope, she experienced the terror of believing she had run in a circle, as an animal will trap itself through panic and exhaustion.

An opening appeared in the trees. She stumbled onto a well-worn track that led to the top of the slope. She drove herself toward the ridge on quivering legs.

Something huge and furry rose from brush and stepped onto the trail above her. With a scream of anguish, pushed beyond the limit of her endurance, she collapsed, sobbing, onto the needle-coated floor of the wooded slope.

THREE

"Didn't mean to give ye sech a scare, ma'am," the grizzled mountain man said.

"I . . . I don't know what I thought. That you were the bear, I suppose."

"I been called worse'n that." The trapper, who had identified himself as one Henry Stallworth, chuckled. Mistaking him for a bear, with his fur cap and full beard and tasseled leather jacket, was not all that farfetched, she thought ruefully. "Ye say ye dropped a pack o' meat. I expect yer grizzly stopped to injoy same. Ye sure ye're feelin' easy now?"

"Yes . . . thanks to you. Now all I want is to reach civilization. It doesn't matter where— wherever you're going."

"Well, we wuz headin' fer Santa Fe. Me and my pardners got some plews to sell, an' some deer skins." His gap-toothed grin included the two Mexican trappers with him in his plans. They were called Antonio Garcia and Carlos Aguilar. Squat, swarthy men with jet black hair, they hardly looked different to Jaine Bryant from many of the Indians she had lived with.

The trappers had seen her fire the night before. In the morning they had started warily in that direction, not sure if it had been an Indian or trapper's fire. It was her cries—and Jaine had been unaware of yelling aloud when she ran from the grizzly—that had drawn the men to her. Otherwise, approaching on opposite sides of the ridge, they might easily have passed each other without knowing.

That possibility made Jaine Bryant shudder with relief.

For the first time she felt safe. She was in the company of three men who seemed to mean her no harm. They were armed men, experienced in traveling through this wilderness. Her chances of escaping from it alive, alone and unarmed, had been minimal. Now everything had changed.

Thank God, she thought. This vast country made it easy to pray.

The trappers shifted some of their gear to free one horse for her. After they had rested for an hour, heating coffee and smoking and asking her how she had come to be alone in the mountains—although they had not prodded deeply, she noticed—they mounted the horses and started south. The going was infinitely easier than it would have been on foot, for they did a great deal of climbing and descending along steep paths. After every climb Jaine thought of what it would have been to cover the same rocky terrain in her moccasins.

Late in the afternoon the party entered a deep valley through which a stream flowed south. They followed the watercourse. The valley was in shadow while the high peaks above remained bathed in brilliant sunshine.

At the far edge of the park they made night camp. The trail ahead was rugged, Henry Stallworth told her. It would best be traveled in full daylight.

Exhausted from the long day, Jaine Bryant fell into her buffalo robe early, while the three trappers sat quietly around the fire, smoking their pipes, talking little. She felt a strong welling of

225

gratitude toward these strangers. Before she could find any words adequate to express the emotion, or decide if the words would simply embarrass them, she slept.

FOUR

The smoke from their campfire, curling out of the shadowed basin into the lighter sky of early evening, caught Angus Haws's alert gaze.

He was returning prematurely to his valley. The trip toward Taos had ended in disaster. On the second day after he had swung south he was seen and followed by renegade Pueblos, outlaws of the forested mountains of the upper Rio Grande del Norte basin since the vindictive counterattack by white soldiers, trappers, and traders against the Taos pueblo more than a year and a half ago had brought the bitter surrender of the Pueblo Indians and their Mexican allies. Some Indians had been hanged. Others had escaped to become outlaws.

As Haws was breaking camp the next morning—the same morning Jaine Bryant abandoned the cave where he had left her—the Pueblos attacked. He retreated to the cover of some rocks and fought them off. His aim with rifle and pistol was deadly, but the Indians had separated him from his two packhorses and run them off. After an hour of shooting, the taking of one white scalp didn't seem worth the heavy cost to the renegades. Two were already dead from Haws's accurate fire. With their booty of pelts and two horses, the surviving Pueblos withdrew. Haws was left with only his personal gear and the big gelding he rode. Luckily he had left his traps behind in the cave, or they would also have been lost.

In bitter anger he turned back, emptyhanded. No need to go to Taos without money or pelts to buy supplies, and it would have been futile as well as dangerous to attempt to pursue the Pueblos.

On the evening of the following day, still a day's ride from his secret valley, he saw the smoke. He went to higher ground and studied it in the failing light. He had no way of knowing whose fire it was, but it disturbed him. It was on the trail north, a way familiar to all mountain men who had worked the beaver waters of these mountains, and it was too close to his valley—and his woman.

He decided to investigate that campfire after dark. It would mean traveling in darkness for an estimated two hours, but he had to know whose fire it was.

During the last hour he moved slowly up a steep canyon watercourse, the narrow trail picking its way along the edge of the tumbling stream. He dismounted and hobbled the gelding far down the canyon. It was unshod, but a hoof could still sound clearly on rock, with the canyon walls to funnel the sound upward. The campfire, he knew now, was at the top of this canyon, at the edge of a wide, circular basin whose floor was deep in summer grass.

The sound of the water rushing down the trough it had carved in the mountain covered Haws's silent approach. Near the top he left the trail and climbed the west wall of the gorge, cautiously feeling his way in the dark. Not a single stone fell.

At the top he crawled across a shoulder of smooth rock and came within sight of the camp.

Haws lay still, a cold fury rising within him. There were three men sitting around the fire. Two were Mexicans. The other was a mountain man. With his bearded face averted, he was hardly distinguishable from an Indian except to one who knew the breed well, who was one of them. The firelight was not enough for Haws to identify him.

A fourth figure, huddled in a buffalo robe beyond the fire, appeared to be sleeping. Haws recognized the spill of golden hair. It was Willow.

Three men, he thought, the cold rage knotting in his belly. Three men who would soon be dead.

Haws moved away. There was no haste in his movements. Each was careful and slow. When he was well away from the camp and no slight sound would betray his presence, he descended to the floor of the basin.

The deep grasses completely concealed him. Even in daylight he would have been undetected as he slithered toward the camp on his belly, his passage as silent as the breeze stirring the thick green cover. He drew within twenty feet of the camp before he lay still.

He heard a soft whisper in Spanish, an answering chuckle. The two Mexicans were half facing him. Both had rifles within reach. The third man had his back to Haws. He was the reason Haws had approached the camp at this point. He was the one least likely to panic, the most dangerous one. He would die first.

No, he would be put down, Haws thought, crippled and disarmed. Haws didn't want the dying to come quickly. Not for him.

Haws inched forward. He carried four weapons: his Hawken rifle, primed and loaded before he moved in; his horse pistol, also ready to fire; his skinning knife in its sheath; and his small shingling hatchet. The latter was an all-purpose tool used for everything from scraping hides to hammering stakes to breaking bones for cooking. It was also a formidable weapon, the Indian's favorite in hand-to-hand fighting.

Haws might have sat off in safe cover and tried to pick off the three men, one by one, with gunfire. He'd rejected the possibility. His first shot would certainly have killed one man, but the other two would have been able to dive out of the circle of light from the fire. If they had then chosen to stay and fight he would have been able to stalk them in the darkness. But what if they had chosen to run? They had their horses nearby. Haws's gelding was far down the canyon. And if they had taken different directions, he would have been able to chase only one.

An Indian would have run their horses off first, and at times like this Haws thought much like an Indian. But he hadn't an Indian's interest in horseflesh for its own sake. If the men got away, an Indian would have been content with stolen horses. Not Haws. He wanted the men themselves. All three of them.

When he was ten feet from the trampled grass that marked the edge of the campsite, Angus Haws slowly gathered himself for the attack. He let his anger out of its cage as an act of will, allowing it to surge through his body and to pound in his brain. *These men stole Willow!* He eased from his prone position until he was in a low crouch. He shifted his rifle into his left hand and tugged his short hatchet from its slot in his belt, hefting it in his right hand.

He attacked in a rush. There was almost no warning until he was there, his small ax raised, ready to strike. Even so the mountain man with his back toward him heard the whisper of danger and tried to evade it. He was rising, turning, when Haws brought the heavy, sharp-edged blade down in a chopping stroke. The honed edge thumped into the white trapper's muscular back. He screamed and toppled forward, bowled off his feet by the force of the blow.

Angus Haws was already turning away, leaving the hatchet buried in his victim's back, knowing that he was not dead but that he was crippled and out of the fight. He would live long enough to suffer and know why he was dying. Haws whipped his rifle waist-high and fired at the nearest of the Mexicans as he reached for his weapon. At a distance of a dozen feet Haws didn't need to aim. The bullet tore into the man's side, smashing bone and flesh. He sprawled sideways onto his face and chest.

Behind Haws, Willow cried out, but he hardly heard her. Dropping his rifle, he pulled his dragoon pistol clear.

But the third man had made his choice when Haws leaped out of the darkness like an avenging angel. Carlos Aguilar had lived too close to death to fail to recognize it when he saw it. Making no try for his rifle, he flung himself over backward into the tall grass and scuttled away in a frantic effort to escape. Haws saw him vanish into the darkness. He took a step after him and suddenly whirled, warned by some instinct.

Henry Stallworth, the hatchet buried in his

231

back, twisting his face into a mask of agony, had managed to seize his rifle. He was trying to bring it up to sight on Haws's back but his hands and arms refused to function. Haws saw the long barrel lifting toward him. He had wanted the trapper alive, but he didn't hesitate. He fired his pistol and saw the mountain man's body jerk from the impact.

Then Haws swung back toward the green darkness into which the remaining Mexican had fled. Haws glided after him. He still had his knife, but he reloaded his pistol as he moved, dropping powder into the barrel and giving it a hard shake to spill powder through the priming hole, wetting a lead ball with his saliva so that it would stick to the powder when he dropped it down the barrel—there was no time to use a patch.

Behind him rose a terrified sobbing, almost a whimper. Willow. Had she betrayed him, then? Had she come willingly with these three trappers? The possibility added fuel to his killing rage.

In the dark, having easily followed the Mexican's blundering path through the grass for some distance away from the camp, Haws paused. He could smell the Mexican. He could smell the sweat of the man's fear. He was still nearby. Haws listened, waiting. Few animals in panic could wait out danger, holding themselves still, making no sound, not even breathing aloud, refusing to break. Man was not usually one of them.

Carlos Aguilar, who had heard Haws tracking him, heard nothing now, and the silence, coming after the brief savagery of that awesome attack upon the camp, broke his nerve. He ran. Fear had wiped away his normal cunning, and the result was that he ran directly away from Haws, toward the center of the tilted meadow—where he could not possibly escape.

When he rose up enough to run at full speed Haws could see him. When he stayed low he was unable to move fast enough. Haws stalked him without concern for his own life. The man fleeing him had no firearm. He had abandoned his rifle, and if he had carried a pistol in his belt he would certainly have fired at his pursuer. No matter which way the Mexican tried to run, Haws quickly spotted him and followed, closing the gap.

Eventually Aguilar stumbled and fell. Rising, he turned to fight, as a cornered rat turns. Angus Haws worked close and stopped, facing him.

"*Hijo de la chingada!*" the Mexican shouted.

Haws shot him in the belly.

He came and stood over Aguilar as he writhed in the tall grass, which was soon slick with his blood. Haws reloaded without haste. He waited until the Mexican trapper went rigid, staring at him with bulging black eyes as Haws aimed his horse pistol at a point directly between the eyes. Then he slowly lowered the pistol.

"Ye kin crawl some," he said. "Ye squaw-stealin' bastard. This child'll be back to see how far ye gits with yer guts spillin' out like that. Ye'll have time to pray ye're dead before I come back fer ye."

He walked away, ignoring the Mexican's screams.

Haws approached the campsite quietly, although he had no reason to fear either Willow or the white trapper he had left twice wounded. There was no sound from the camp. When he reached it, he saw the woman sitting up, her legs folded under her to one side. She was hunched over and rocking slightly, the way an Indian woman grieved.

Then Haws let out a bellow of rage.

The white mountain man was gone.

FIVE

When Henry Stallworth rose to meet Haws's attack, he had a passing contempt for his own stupidity. The woman was a runaway. Why hadn't he given more thought to the possibility that Angus Haws might return unexpectedly?

Stallworth knew Haws, as all mountain men

knew of each other. He knew Haws to be dangerous if angered.

Chivalry, he thought. God save a man from
being both chivalrous and foolish.

All this flashed through his mind in the instant
he sensed a presence behind him, hearing with
a wilderness man's keen ears the stirring of
leathers, the slide of a moccasin in wet grass. He
was turning and ducking as he rose, instinctively
trying to slide away from the assault. Because
he was, the hatchet buried itself in the thick hard
pack of muscle behind his left shoulder instead
of crushing his spine.

His whole brain seemed to turn into a white
pudding. He found himself on the ground without awareness of how he had fallen. He tried to
reach the ax but half of his body was paralyzed.
He couldn't reach around far enough.

He heard the explosion of Haws's rifle and the
whack of the bullet tearing into a man's body.
Whose? Garcia's? Aguilar's?

A man who had lived in the wilderness with
his rifle and his knife close to his hand learned to
react by instinct. In the instant of waking alarmed
his hand closed on knife hilt or gun butt. That
instinct ruled Henry Stallworth now in spite of
his agony. His right hand closed on his rifle and
dragged it near. He struggled to face Haws, who
was crossing the clearing, stepping past a corner
of the fire, moving after Carlos Aguilar. Antonio

Garcia was lying face down. Stallworth knew that he was dead even though he couldn't see him clearly.

He couldn't see Haws clearly either, but at that distance he wouldn't have needed to. The trouble was that he couldn't seem to lift his rifle clear of the ground. Instinct could only carry him so far. It couldn't supply strength or counteract a hatchet stuck in his back.

Angus Haws heard his panting struggle. When he turned he had his horse pistol in his hand. For some reason Stallworth didn't hear the crash of the pistol. He felt the heavy tug of the bullet as it smashed into his side.

He lost consciousness briefly. When it returned he seemed to be swimming in a sea of mud. It was wet and black and thick, and he couldn't get anywhere with his feeble paddling.

After a while—he didn't know if it was minutes or seconds—rational thought returned. Haws had fired hastily. For the second time Stallworth's life had been spared, at least temporarily. The bullet had struck his ribs on a glancing course, ricocheting off bone instead of penetrating. It had taken a sheath of flesh and skin and maybe some splinters, and there was already considerable bleeding, but the lead ball had not struck anything vital and it had gone on its way. He was still alive.

Maybe, soon enough, he would wish he weren't.

With a costly effort Stallworth reached over his shoulder with his right hand and grasped the handle of the hatchet. Sweat stood out on his face. He gave a violent wrench. The blade pulled free.

The trapper moaned softly between set jaws. Once more he dropped into the black pool.

This time he didn't go under all the way. This time he was certain that only seconds passed before he was thinking again, and his thoughts, insofar as they were formulated thoughts at all, concentrated solely on survival. He didn't look at the woman, who stared after him, in her eyes the distant look of shock. He dragged his rifle with him, and he hadn't done that consciously. He crawled across an edge of the fire and started a small patch of flame on his leggings. He didn't feel it, and as he crawled on it was smothered.

When he was beyond the clearing he tried to get to his feet. He fell down and rose again. His body was lean and hard and tough, and it could endure an astonishing amount of punishment. Before long he was covering several yards between falls.

The ground disappeared under his feet and he fell headlong into the river. After the first shock he was seized by a wild exhilaration. The icy water cleared his brain. Moreover, the noisy rush over the rocky bed would cover any sounds he made. And he wouldn't leave tracks if he could keep to the stream and avoid drowning.

The night turned darker. He felt panic, thinking that he was passing out again. But he had stumbled into the mouth of the canyon. The dark was only the high walls shutting off most of the light from the starlit sky.

He was on a descending grade. That made it easier to keep moving, but he fell heavily twice more. The second time, when he tried to rise he felt astonishment. Nothing happened. He was unable to get up.

He lay at the edge of the stream, almost submerged. From far away came Angus Haws's bellows of rage.

Twice in the next hour Haws prowled close by without seeing him. He was protected by the deep shadows at the canyon bottom and partly by Haws's own fury. It drove him down the canyon the first time on the run. When he returned he was still hurrying, afraid that Stallworth had escaped him in some other direction.

Henry Stallworth lay in the water for two hours. The ice-cold waters stopped his bleeding and cleansed his wounds. When he finally struggled erect on weak, shaking legs, after a long period of silence had made him think Haws was searching elsewhere, probably quartering the meadow over and over, he was able to stay on his feet.

He didn't think of going back, or of trying to ambush Haws. His rifle and powder were wet, and he knew that he couldn't trust his ability to clean and dry and load the weapon even if some of the powder in his horn had stayed dry. And if he did all that and the weapon fired at all, his aim was not to be relied on. Not when one shot meant his life or death.

His only chance to stay alive, and that a slim one, was to get far enough away before it was light and Haws could begin tracking him.

Halfway down the long descent he came upon Angus Haws's gelding.

SIX

Toward noon of the following day Haws found the gelding nibbling peacefully in an open meadow beside the stream.

When he had left the horse and the beaten trail, Henry Stallworth had chosen his escape route carefully. He had followed a narrow sheep trail that climbed toward an irregular ridge to the east. If Haws followed him up that tight trail, he had to fear walking into the muzzle of a rifle with no way to hide from it. And if Haws took the time to climb to that ridge some other way, he might only find that Stallworth had struck off in any of a dozen different directions.

Moreover, Haws could only follow on foot. The track was too narrow for any horse to climb. He would have to leave his gelding behind, along with the five horses he had claimed from Stallworth and his dead companions.

And he would have to leave the woman behind or drag her along with him.

In the end Angus Haws turned angrily north toward his hidden valley. Willow, her face swollen and discolored from the single, silent, vicious blow Haws had dealt out to punish her betrayal, rode sullenly behind.

10 / The Hidden Valley

ONE

"You think he'll live, Tom?" Ter Bryant asked.

"This child never seed any man deader was still makin' sense."

"Does that mean yes or no?"

Tom Brock shrugged. "If that hatchet didn't kill him, making one big hole in his back, and if gettin' shot didn't kill him, and breaking his jaw so he no could chew, and crawlin' out of them mountains the way he done, then I don't suppose lyin' on his back and drinkin' fort rum will put him under."

They had made camp in the shadows of the Sangre de Cristo range, their route penetrating northwest into the mountains west of El Pueblo, bypassing the higher peaks. Restless now that he was denied the solace of punishing activity, Bryant's thoughts turned to the story of Angus Haws's attack on the three trappers who had rescued Jaine. It was a tale that Henry Stallworth had told painfully, gritting out each word after his broken jaw had been wired in place. The jaw, ironically, had not been broken in the fight

241

with Haws. Stallworth had fallen down a small cliff during his grueling two-month flight from the mountains—half of which time had been lost in hiding or recuperating from his other wounds. The fact that he had made it out of the wilderness to tell his tale still seemed incredible. His rifle had been damaged. Unable to shoot game, he had subsisted on roots and wild berries. Gradually weakening, he had been reduced to a crawl at the last. Stallworth had been driven by a desperate will to survive, but Ter Bryant knew that he would always be grateful to the man.

Now, brooding beside his campfire, Bryant recalled the words Stallworth had kept repeating. "He's crazy, that Haws. I tell ye, he's taken the weed. He's gone loco."

Crazy, maybe, but as dangerous as a maddened grizzly. Haws had killed two men without warning to get Jaine back, and the third had escaped only by lucky circumstance.

The danger made Bryant glad enough to have Tom Brock along, but at the same time he was reluctant to have Brock risk his neck. There had been no way around it. As self-reliant as Bryant had become during his year and a half on the plains, he lacked Brock's knowledge of the mountains. The description of the area where Jaine had stumbled out of the wilderness, and of the hidden valley she had spoken of to the trappers, meant nothing to him. For Brock the former at least was like a mark on a map.

And, truth to tell, Brock had not hesitated. "It's not your fight, Tom," Bryant had said. "Just find him for me, that's all. Then he's mine."

Brock had grunted scornfully. "You think this child go hunt a crazy man jist for you? *Mais non, mon ami*. It is for her, for Madame Bryant. We find her together, eh?"

The mountain man's code said that a man looked out for himself, fought his own fights, defended his own, be it his woman or his horse or his personals. But Bryant knew that Tom Brock was making this his own fight as well, out of friendship or simply because Jaine had, as he once said softly, "treat this child fine."

Bryant tried to think of Haws without the haze of anger, as a hunter seeks to know his quarry. He did not let himself fall into the trap of thinking about Jaine's relationship with the mountain man.

"What kind of man is he, Tom? What made him come out West? What makes him hide out in these mountains?"

"He come like de rest of us. *Pourquoi*? Maybe he don't like it where he was."

"But he's different. You were like him once, maybe, you and Old Bill and Dick Wootton and the others. But you all gave it up. You said yourself the beaver isn't worth the trouble of skinning any more. What makes a man like Haws

243

go on alone? Is he crazy, like Stallworth says? Is he just plain loco?"

For a long time Tom Brock was silent. The silence of the high peaks and the night forests and the great plains seemed to get inside a man who had lived long in such surroundings. Brock and Haws were two such men.

"It all be changed," Brock said after a while, and it seemed that he wasn't answering Bryant's question but musing aloud. "It was different then. You had to be there to know how she was. This child remember it. Likely Haws remember it, too. They was beaver like you never seed, lad. They jist jumped into de traps, it seemed like. There wasn't all de wagons comin' then, not like now. There wasn't nobody but us and de Injuns and de beaver and de grizzly bear. When we come to de rendezvous, *mon ami*, it was some, I tell you! Whiskey and them squaws, and suckin' a beaver tail or a boudie, fiddlin' and stompin' and fightin', it was like we had somethin' no child ever had before. And maybe we thought it would be like that all time forever.

"It be different now," he repeated, talking longer than Bryant had ever heard him. "De beaver, she's worthless, no good trapping her, but some trapper, he can't go back. Haws be like that. They's other men like him in de mountains. Maybe Haws be crazy. Maybe he jist be gittin' back at de world for changin', for not stayin' like she was. Ain't no way of sayin' for certain, lad, what be in that child's mind. Only one thing matter. He got your woman, and he won't give her up to you."

Ter Bryant stared at him across the low campfire, mildly surprised by the long speech. He mulled it over without comment, hardly aware that something of the land's long silences had got into him, too. When he came to Tom Brock's simple conclusion, he saw its wisdom. Brock was telling him to forget the rest, forget Henry Stallworth's speculations or his own, think only about what you have to do.

Haws wanted Jaine. The fact didn't surprise Bryant. What man could know her long without wanting her? What man could have her and willingly give her up?

"He waitin' for you," Tom Brock said. "He knows you's comin'. Only one way you gits your woman back, *mon ami*. You got to kill him."

TWO

The sense of urgency grew as the two men worked deeper into the mountains. There was the possibility to face that Angus Haws might not have returned to his valley. Expecting or fearing pursuit, he might have struck off for some more distant, unknown retreat. There was the chance that, even if Haws had returned to that valley with Jaine, its opening would prove elusive, even impossible to find. And there were the mountains themselves, for winter came early here, and already it was well into September. Early snows would obliterate all sign, hide or block the passes, force the searchers to struggle for their own survival.

Tom Brock had recognized the description of the park and canyon where Henry Stallworth had escaped Haws's vengeance. Here he and Bryant came a week after leaving Pueblo. After two months of intervening sun and rain there was little evidence of the campsite, but near the head of the canyon the two searchers found the skeletal remains of a man's body, the bones picked clean by scavengers. A search of the meadow failed to turn up the body of the other Mexican trapper.

Now Bryant knew that he was close to Haws's secret valley. According to Stallworth's account, and what he had heard from Jaine, that valley was not much more than a day's ride to the north.

The two men pushed on through the afternoon and evening. With the coming of full darkness they made cold camp under an overcast sky. It seemed unlikely that Haws would have kept a nightly vigil for two months, but they avoided a fire nevertheless.

In the morning Bryant woke while it was still dark. The air was bitter cold, the sky black. He found himself wishing that he could risk heating coffee while he waited for first light. Then he damned himself for the yearning.

In the darkness he was hardly aware that it had begun to snow, so light was the fall. He felt moisture on his eyelids and his lips but thought it only morning mist. After a few minutes the pale white coating on the ground began to appear.

"Tom! Tom, God damn it, it's snowing!"

Brock was awake at once, but there was nothing to do but wait for daylight.

In the hour between those first drifting flakes and the arrival of dawn a thin layer of snow was dropped over the mountains. Daylight revealed a world of fresh, pure beauty. The pines on the slopes and covering the ridge where they had camped were dusted with white. The high peaks were lost in a whirling curtain. The open basin below them to the west was transformed into a calm white sea.

Across that white emptiness there was now no single track to be seen.

THREE

It was Tom Brock who suggested that they split up. Guided by worn hollows, broken branches, trampled grass or cleared lanes through brush and trees, the two men had spent the morning following old animal or Indian trails, casting back and forth over a series of ridges and valleys west of their night camp. A light snow continued to fall, but the sky was brightening. The clouds over the peaks were thinner and higher, suggesting that the storm was already weakening and would not last through the day. It had already done its damage.

At noon they had a cold meal of hardtack and jerky washed down with water. They were in a sheltered depression between two ridges. Brock believed they were close to the place where the trappers had found Jaine. The parallel ridges funneled the eye toward a saddle peak directly to the north. Stallworth had not mentioned this landmark, but it would help the two men to return to this spot as a meeting place.

"A man lookin' for beaver, he want to find him some quiet water," Brock said. "These mountains has many such, but some time they's not easy to find. We find her sooner if we looks two ways."

It was agreed that Brock would explore the seemingly impassable heights to the south, searching for an opening. Bryant would range farther west where some notched hills were visible beyond the flat-topped ridge.

"We comes back here afore dark," Brock suggested. "The saddle mountain, she make good landmark. You find Haws's valley, it be best if you no go in *solitaire, mon ami.* We meets here."

Although Bryant nodded, there was a hard eagerness in his eyes that did not surprise the older man. Driven by his angry hatred and worried about the snow that covered all trails, Bryant was not in a mood for caution.

When they parted Tom Brock rode toward the bluffs south of their camp. He watched his friend disappear into timber as he crossed the nearby ridge. When Bryant was well out of sight, Brock's gaze swung thoughtfully toward the rock cliffs facing him. There was a line running at an upward angle across one steep mountain. It disappeared for a while, then appeared again some distance to the right, continuing the same angle of ascent. To a less experienced eye it did not even look like a trail, for it was almost completely hidden by the fresh snow; Ter Bryant had missed it. But Tom Brock had glimpsed places high along that thread where it became a ledge worn smooth over centuries of use. That track had to lead somewhere.

Brock's guess was that it led to the entrance into Angus Haws's hidden valley.

He rode slowly, letting his horse pick its own way along the narrow path. In an hour he had reached the split in the mountain that wasn't a split at all but two separate faces of rock, one set back from the other so that the opening between them wasn't visible until you were standing in the gates.

Dismounting at the mouth of the pass, Brock considered the trail ahead. No more than six feet wide, at places narrower, it suggested an ideal place for an ambush. But would Haws expect pursuit after all this time? Would he expect it at all, knowing how badly Henry Stallworth had been hurt?

The walls of the pass offered little concealment. Though fissured here and there, sometimes sheer, sometimes broken by falls of rock, dotted by occasional scrub pines growing where they had no right to grow, they seemed impossible to climb.

He would go in part way, Brock decided. If he didn't like the look of things, he would turn back and wait for his young friend. At least he would have made sure that Bryant didn't charge in blindly on his own.

And if the way into the valley seemed clear, well, Tom Brock knew that he stood a far better chance to come out alive in a tangle with Angus Haws than Bryant did.

The lad would be angry, Brock thought. No matter.

He left his horse hobbled and entered the pass on foot, making no sound on the snow-covered floor of the gorge. The trail twisted and turned, changing little, until, at a point he judged to be about halfway through the mountain, it suddenly broadened out. Here the floor was ten yards or more across, and a small stand of stubby pines grew along one side.

Tom Brock studied this opening for several minutes in silence, hugging the canyon wall and exposing himself as little as possible. At last he was satisfied. There was no danger here.

Beyond the wider opening the pass narrowed again, but its slot framed a glimpse of open sky ahead and a thread of green that might be the tops of trees. Feeling excitement quicken, Brock steeled himself against it. Slower now, lad. If he's waiting, this will be the spot.

He crossed the open shelf without incident, reaching what seemed the safer narrowing of the gorge. He relaxed a little.

A man who has passed a place of danger safely will tend to relax a little. Angus Haws had banked on that. The first glimpse of the valley ahead tempted the eye, luring it from the immediate trail. Haws had known that, too. Even so his trap might have failed if it hadn't been for the snow.

To Tom Brock's keen eye even the slightest disturbance in the dust on the floor of the pass would have been a clear warning. He would have noticed an area too clean, as if a leafy branch had been used to wipe away sign. But now an inch of snow covered everything. Even the tips of the branches of a scrub pine growing out of the wall, where missing needles would ordinarily have caught his eye, were now uniformly dusted with the soft white powder snow.

The trap had been placed in the narrow slot of the trail a few feet past the opening Brock had studied so carefully.

He sensed danger as his foot was coming down. There was nothing specific to alert him. Set into a shallow trench, the heavy steel trap—it was a bear trap with double springs and a circular base, powerful enough to bite through a man's leg—was completely invisible under its double layers of dust and snow. But either Brock's senses or some indefinable wilderness instinct sounded an alarm. As his foot nudged the edge of the trap he tried to pull back. He heard the harsh slam of steel jaws and felt a chill of fear as he leaped away. The steel teeth caught only moccasin leather and skin.

But Haws had counted on that as well. He had counted on his prey reacting as the beaver did, diving toward safety when the trap was sprung. Tom Brock's lunge carried him against the gnarled little pine clinging to the wall of the pass. Its snow-covered branches concealed a stout bent branch that sprang free under the pressure of Brock's weight, triggering a second trap—a deadfall set above the trail.

As if released from a chute, a small avalanche of rocks crashed down upon Long Tom Brock.

He had no chance to escape it. The delicately balanced pile had seemed part of the canyon wall, and his gaze, roving ahead toward the valley, had missed it. One of the first big rocks broke his shoulder. By chance the spill smashed him backward instead of burying him completely. The bulk of the stones pinned the lower half of his body, crushing both legs.

In an agony of pain that tore no sound from his blood-flecked lips, Long Tom lay helpless on the floor of the pass, half-buried. He was still alive then, and conscious.

The thunder of the rock slide penetrated deep into the valley, but it was an hour before Angus Haws stood on the far side of the pile, listening.

Tom Brock saw a small gleam of bright blue peering at him from a gap in the rocks near the top of the pile. It disappeared in the instant he saw it, but Haws had seen enough. A moment later he climbed over the fall. He descended without haste to the floor of the pass, dislodging a few loose rocks under his weight, starting miniature slides.

He stared down at the black man. After a moment he said, "Ye ain't the one."

No, Brock said, but no sound emerged.

Angus Haws nodded. "He'll be comin' soon then."

Slowly he drew his skinning knife from its sheath.

FOUR

At dusk Ter Bryant returned to the appointed meeting place. It was full dark before he began to believe that Tom Brock wasn't coming. By then it was too late to hunt for him. Either he had found the valley and gone in or something had happened to him. Or both.

The next day dawned bright and clear. The storm was over. The sky was a brilliant blue, the mountains so dazzling in their snow cover that Byrant's eyes were soon aching from the glare.

The trail Tom Brock had left behind the day before had been partially covered by later snow, but there were enough disturbances visible for Bryant to follow the tracks easily. Once he had found the path that climbed upward toward the opening in the mountain he no longer needed Brock's sign.

He found Tom's horse at the mouth of the pass and turned him loose. Nickering gratefully, the horse followed him into the clean hard shadows at the bottom of the gorge. After a short distance Bryant dismounted. He walked cautiously forward, holding his own horse's reins. The deeper he went the more he could feel danger closing around him like the waters of a dark pool. Heart hammering, he finally let the reins go and carried his rifle ready in both hands.

The pass widened out abruptly. He saw the stand of trees along the right side of the opening and judged them empty, but his glance there was fleeting. Almost instantly it was riveted on the fall of rocks blocking the way past the clearing.

Tom Brock's body lay crucified upon the rocks. The legs had been crushed—caught in the slide, Bryant guessed. It was the only clear thought he had before anguish engulfed him. Tom's nose and ears had been cut off, the lower body gutted and disemboweled.

The message was savagely clear. Angus Haws knew he was coming. This was what he had done to a man far more skilled and dangerous a fighter than Ter Bryant.

If Bryant came on, he would die in the same way, slowly and horribly.

The afternoon passed in aching, mind-numbing grief. Ter Bryant covered it with activity as best he could. He wrapped Tom Brock's body in his blanket and laboriously sewed the covering together to make a tight cocoon. Then he rolled this bundle into Tom's ground sheet. Gently he laid his friend at the foot of the rock spill at the edge of the clearing.

For more than an hour he shifted rocks. He wore gloves for the work, but by the end his gloves were cut and torn, his lacerated fingers bleeding. By then he had partially cleared the blockage. And Tom Brock lay buried under a monument of the stones that had trapped him.

When all this was done Bryant rested. Now he could no longer hide from his sorrow. He thought of the long months he and Tom had ridden together, the scrapes they had been through, the frustrating search they had shared.

Once Brock had said that he was born on the French Caribbean island of Guadeloupe, where his ancestors had been slaves, then free, then re-enslaved. His mother had helped him to flee the island when he was a boy. Somehow he had found his way safely to the mainland, and then to a ship that sailed around the Horn and eventually to an Oregon port. There Brock had found the land where he could be free, where he could make of himself whatever he chose.

That was all Tom Brock had ever revealed about his past. How little he really knew of Tom, Bryant thought, and yet how much of everything that mattered, for he knew of Brock's courage and loyalty, his coolness under fire, his easy humor, his friendship.

And he knew that Tom Brock had died for him, trying to save him from the same fate.

It was something for Ter Bryant to remember when he came face to face with Angus Haws.

FIVE

After dark Bryant crept over the rock slide and started down the pass. He had studied it for a long time as the late afternoon turned into twilight, making sure that he had the canyon's contours printed in his mind.

He expected a trap. After a lifetime of taking beaver and other animals, Haws's mind surely worked that way. After weighing the advantages of darkness against the risk of blundering blindly into another of Angus Haws's snares, he had decided that the cover for his own movements was worth the risk.

Once in the valley he would have freedom to move about. He wouldn't be forced along any particular baited track. He would be able to fight Haws at a distance. A man was a fool to try arm-locking with a grizzly, or to pit newly gained wilderness skills against the man who had outwitted Long Tom.

But first he had to get into the valley.

The sky was mostly clear that night. Although the floor of the canyon was dark as a dungeon, the walls above his head were thrown into relief against the paler darkness of the night sky. As Bryant inched down the pass he studied these walls constantly for any unnatural bulge or change in outline. He doubted that Haws would repeat the same kind of trap that had caught Tom

Brock, but he watched for it all the same. He had seen the deadfall used in Mississippi to trap animals, and he'd heard tales of the way robbers along the Natchez Trace had used it to catch human prey.

He also tested each foot of the canyon floor, riding a long stick along the bottom ahead of him, its scratches muffled by the light snow.

The stick failed to trigger any trap. The canyon offered no other hazard. After a taut hour, progressing foot by foot, Bryant saw the walls moving away from him, the pass opening out ahead. He had reached the entrance to Haws's valley.

Here the risk of trap or ambush seemed magnified. Wouldn't Haws want to keep him confined in the canyon rather than loose in the valley?

He studied the heights on either side, searching for hand- and footholds, a way to climb. The walls were more broken and irregular as the canyon opened out. After a few moments' search he discovered a series of narrow, perpendicular fissures that enabled him to climb onto a massive shoulder of rock. He wormed his way over this hump until he was able once again to look down into the valley.

It was a huge, dark bowl, perhaps a mile across, its far reaches out of sight toward the south. The surface of a lake along the east side of the bowl gleamed silver in the light of moon and stars, and here and there a number of silvery threads of streams glittered. Open stretches of meadow were light in color, snow-covered. At least two-thirds of the valley floor was covered by stretches of pine forest, these areas darker, the snow on tree branches creating a lacy filigree instead of an even blanket.

All was peaceful and still.

Somewhere nearby Jaine slept. So close now. If he lifted his head and hollered she would hear him. She would hear his voice and its echo reverberating in the hollow of the bowl. She would know that, at long last, he had found her.

The temptation was strong. Ter Bryant lay quietly on his belly above the entrance to the valley, letting the desire subside.

The gates of the pass were perhaps two hundred feet above the floor of the basin. He tried to follow the trail that led downward. It went left, eastward, soon disappearing into the deceptive night shadows. If that was the only way down, he thought, it would be all too easy to watch.

He studied the drop to the right of this path. Some of it was a sheer precipice, but there were places lower down where tall pines grew as high as the trail. If he could find a way to lower himself, screened by those trees . . .

After a while Bryant eased away from the rim and climbed back down to the canyon floor.

He turned back the way he had come, moving quickly now, sure of his way, no longer worried about buried steel jaws waiting to spring shut.

He found his own and Tom Brock's horse waiting in the clearing beyond the deadfall. Bryant had cleared away enough of the rocks to create a narrow passage. One by one he led the two horses through. Then, holding the reins of both animals, he returned to the mouth of the canyon overlooking the valley.

He sent Brock's mare down first, giving her a whack across the rump to get her started along the descending path. There was both water and forage below, and the mare would soon sense it.

Once started she kept moving. For a while Bryant was able to hear the soft clop of hoofs along the trail. Then the sounds faded away. The mare was no longer visible, hidden by turns in the path and by intervening humps of earth and rock.

Bryant studied the floor below, waiting. Nothing happened. The mare did not appear. As time passed he began to grow anxious. Had Haws caught her? Had she simply stopped? Or was she turning back, wanting company?

Then he saw her, a dark shape moving across a field of snow at a trot. She slowed, stopped, bent her long neck toward the ground. Then she moved on once more. She was working toward the lake.

Was the way clear, then? Or had Haws, watching below, seen that the mare was riderless?

If he had, he would be waiting for a second horse—and its rider.

Slowly Ter Bryant started down the narrow trail, leading his black horse, having to keep a tight hold on the horse's eagerness. Their cautious progress muffled any sounds of movement. About halfway down, at a sharp turn in the path, Bryant stopped. He stood for a long minute, listening. The valley remained still, sleeping under its snow blanket.

Bryant fumbled for his rawhide lariat. He let it out, dropping one end over the cliff face that plummeted toward the floor below. The rope wasn't long enough to reach all the way, but the tall pines Bryant had spotted earlier reached almost as high as the trail at this point. They grew part way up the steep slope.

He searched for a place to secure the other end of the rope near the rim. He rejected some scrub pines and dubious edges of rock, but he was soon in luck. He found a notched hump that seemed a part of the solid wall of the mountain. He worked the lariat tightly into the notch and tied it off. It would hold his weight.

When he was ready he turned the black loose. "Go on," he murmured softly. "She's waitin' for you down there." He gave the horse a slap, and he trotted off.

Bryant got down on his belly and eased over the edge of the cliff.

As he descended on the rope, bracing his feet against the cliff face, he was soon screened by the tops of the pines, as he had hoped. But the thought came before he was far along, suspended on a thin rawhide line, moving out of starlight into a shadowed mystery below, that Angus Haws was not a man to be fooled by any such simple tricks with horses. Even now he might be looking up, watching Bryant from the darkness, smiling and waiting. The thought brought a chill that struck far deeper than the night's freezing cold.

But then he was far down among the pines, the narrow trail lost from sight overhead, the slope suddenly pushing against his feet as it angled away from the cliff. He let his weight ease off the rope. A snow-heavy branch brushed against him, white powder sifting through the air. Sliding and scrambling over the lower slope, Bryant reached level ground and the safe darkness of the pine forest.

Quickly he moved away from the cliff, melting into the shadows of the trees.

Now he could only hide, and wait for the day to come.

11 / Bait for a Trap

ONE

Angus Haws had recognized Long Tom Brock from the old days, the early years of trapping. The fact had not kept him from killing the helpless man without remorse, torturing him cruelly. In his anger at this invasion of his valley, the attempt to steal his woman, he had taken pleasure in the dying man's suffering.

But Brock was a black man, an old trapper rather than an emigrant. He was not the husband Willow had spoken of, the man who searched for her.

That one would follow soon. The warning Haws left, Brock's dead body spread-eagled across the deadfall, was not intended to stop the man but to instill fear, to unnerve and intimidate him. A frightened prey was more vulnerable.

Haws made no attempt to block the pass completely. Let the man Bryant come. Let him get close, quaking in his Eastern boots. In the end he would walk into another trap as clumsily as the black man. He wouldn't be able to avoid it. Haws meant to set out bait Bryant would be unable to resist.

Willow was in the cave. Twice since her recapture she had tried to leave. Each time Haws had beaten her. Oddly, she did not cower from his blows. Her silence, her refusal to cringe or whimper, evoked grudging respect in the mountain man.

This was no porcelain doll. Haws wanted her as his wife, finally and completely. That would be possible only when the other man was dead. Haws was glad that he had finally come. Soon Willow would have no reason to run away. In time she would be content. Haws was quite certain of that.

Nevertheless he remained angry with her. When he had left for Taos he had half convinced himself that she would not try to run away, not only because she feared the wilderness but because she didn't want to leave. No longer could he keep up that pretense. She had tried to escape. At first he had told himself that the three trappers had discovered her in his valley. Now he admitted that she had fled on her own, for on his return he had found no sign of the men entering the valley.

That night in the cave Angus Haws told Willow about the black man who lay dead in the pass. He saw her flinch, hurt more by these words than by his recent blows.

"Poor Tom!"

"That was his name. I taken it ye knew him then."

"Yes. Yes, damn you. You'd no cause to kill him."

"He come after you," Haws said indifferently. " 'Twas his choosin'. The other'll come soon. He'll die, too."

He saw her eyes widen with fear. A flame burned in them, reflecting the light of the fire near the cave mouth. The reaction stung Haws. It was not the pity she had shown for Long Tom Brock but something more, a deeper feeling. He had a glimpse into something he had never known, and the knowledge brought an unreasoning rage so sudden and strong he wanted to strike her, to drive that expression from her eyes. For some reason he refrained.

Instead he said, "Mebbe he'll come tomorrow. Mebbe it'll be the next day. Then it'll be over, and ye'll be mine."

"Let him go," she said suddenly. "I won't run away again. I'll promise you that. Take me away from here now, and I'll be yours as much as I could ever be, if you'll let him live."

As she pleaded for Bryant's life his anger deepened, each word making the man's death more certain. In the end Haws told her harshly to be quiet.

That night he had not reset his traps. In the

morning he again ignored them. Before leaving the cave he bound Willow hand and foot, no longer able to trust her. Then he began a methodical search in the wooded area below the cave for exactly the right place to set the trap he had devised in his mind after long thought.

When he was satisfied that he had found what he wanted, a narrow open strip in the woods that was visible from the cave through its screen of pines, he worked quickly and surely. He had located two tall pines that stood about ten feet apart on either side of the cleared area. Climbing each tree in turn, he cut a sturdy branch short, peeling away the bark and sharpening the end of the section of branch that was left. The two cut branches would have to support between them a weight of around a hundred pounds. Then he cut several heavier poles into short lengths, using his hatchet to sharpen both ends of each piece. He had to cut holes through the earth's frozen crust with the ax before he could pound these sturdy stakes into the ground securely. When he had resharpened the projecting ends he had a staggered double row of sharp stakes pointing skyward across the space between the two pine trees.

When he was done he examined the results. He was satisfied it would work. Later in the day he would prepare and thoroughly wet down several lengths of rawhide thongs. That was all he would need.

He made no effort to cover his tracks in the snow, which was melting under a sunny sky. This was a trap that was meant to be seen. The man Bryant would come to it knowingly, aware of the danger but unable to stay away.

Haws knew he would come to the bait. If he had needed any other assurance than his own cunning, he had seen it in Willow's eyes in that moment of fear. Bryant would come, and Haws would be waiting for him, and it was fitting that the woman would be part of it, that she would participate in his death.

Before noon Haws was at the entrance to the pass. He found no fresh tracks. Bryant had not yet come through the canyon.

He would be delayed, Haws thought, when he found his partner's body.

The reminder made the mountain man frown. What kind of a man was it who inspired that look in Willow's eyes, and the kind of friendship that would make another man die in his place?

Angus Haws waited until dusk. The man did not appear. Returning to the cave, Haws released the woman so that she could prepare his evening meal. Before he lay down to sleep that night on his bed of boughs and buffalo robes, he tied Willow up again.

He knew that this was the last time such

precautions would be needed. Tomorrow, certainly, perhaps even this night under cover of darkness, the man would come.

TWO

Waiting in the cold darkness for dawn to arrive, hunched down with his back against a tree, Ter Bryant thought with bitter regret of Tom Brock's death, and of its meaning. Almost certainly Brock had guessed where the pass into the valley was before he sent him away on a pointless search to the west. The reason was obvious. Tom thought he had a better chance against Haws. Perhaps he had even come to share something of Bryant's hatred of the mountain man.

He'd been wrong to go it alone. Their chances would have been better if they had stuck together. But Tom Brock's unspoken conviction was plain: Ter Bryant would have to be lucky to come out alive in a clash with Haws.

Maybe. But Haws had had to be lucky, too, to catch Tom the way he did. Would it have happened that way if it hadn't snowed the night before? One man's luck could turn, Bryant thought, and another man could get lucky.

There were too many things to think about when you had to wait like this. Luck, and what Haws had done to Tom before he died. Jaine, and what she was feeling now if she knew what was happening. What kind of man Angus Haws was and what had made him that way. And himself. Too many thoughts about himself, too many questions that always came back to whether or not he could beat Haws.

Soon none of the thinking and wondering would matter. It wouldn't matter that the decline of the beaver trade had turned a man like Haws bitter, even a little crazy. It wouldn't matter that cool Tom Brock had turned foolhardy because he loved, or Haws crazy because he loved, or Jaine and Ter Bryant reckless and romantic because they loved. It would all come down to two men facing each other because each wanted the same woman. What was it Jaine had said? Two bucks on a hill, locking horns. And it didn't matter which one the waiting female had taken to her heart.

Let it come, then, Bryant thought. Let it come soon.

When the peaks that defined the valley's eastern wall slowly took shape in the first gray light, while the shadows in the pine forest along the valley floor were still deep and dark, Ter Bryant began his search. The sky brightened, the light caught the high bluffs to the west and stole downward. He moved back and forth, working south, looking for recent tracks or

269

evidence of a beaten path. He went from tree to tree, hardly visible when his shadow merged with that of a tree trunk. He scanned the woods on all sides, listening, reaching out with all his senses, wishing that his heart wouldn't drum so loudly.

The sun shouldered suddenly over the eastern rim, turning the mountain lake from iron gray to an intense blue, the open meadows into dazzling sheets of white. Some of that snow had melted the day before, the rest might go today. The sky was cloudless, the first touch of the sun warm against Bryant's face when he darted across a clearing. The forest floor remained cool in its shade. The snow would linger longer there.

He saw the tracks. They cut through the woods from east to west and back, leading across the valley from the lake toward the western bluffs.

For several minutes he stood motionless, studying the trail, trying to assess it. Then he heard a distant, muffled scream. It cut off suddenly. Bryant felt the hairs rise on the back of his neck.

He tried to place the sound. Ahead of him. Off to the right. His impulse was to run toward it as fast as he could. Was that what Haws wanted? Had he planned it—forced that cry from Jaine?

With abrupt decision Bryant started toward the western wall of the valley. He ran more swiftly now, recklessly, using the cover the woods offered but careless of noise or momentary exposure.

When he reached the bluffs he climbed over tumbled rocks at their foot, trying to get as high as possible. He managed to climb perhaps twenty feet up before he confronted a sheer, unbroken wall. He could see little beyond the immediate area. He had to find another place where he could climb higher.

He was turning back when his eye was caught by something farther along the cliffs to the south. He peered hard, squinting, not sure what had seemed important.

Then he saw it again: a wisp of smoke. It didn't seem enough for a real fire. It was more like the thread a gust of wind might have teased out of a fire that had died—or was supposed to have been put out. Sometimes a coal would stay alive under the ashes like that, and find brief life when a breeze blew over it.

The smoke was gone now. It was almost possible to believe that his eyes had been tricked by the play of sunlight over those irregular bluffs. Almost. Ter Bryant knew he hadn't made a mistake, even though that whiff of smoke had come from what appeared to be a solid wall of rock.

He moved forward as far as he could find footing along the base of the cliff. Leaning out, he saw a horizontal line in the steep face about fifty yards away, a slash that hadn't been visible before. A moment's study told him more. It was a ledge. The smoke had come from there. That meant a man-made fire. Very probably it also meant a cave.

From the forest below, screened by the tall pines that grew close to the narrow ledge, it wouldn't have been visible. Seeing that brief plume of smoke had been chance, pure luck. From any other angle or position Bryant wouldn't have been able to see it or the presence of a cave.

But the cry he had heard—a woman's cry—hadn't come from that high up. It had come from somewhere in the pines below the ledge.

From a place in view of that cave, Bryant thought.

Then he understood. Jaine was in trouble. Haws meant him to know it. He was using her as bait for a trap. There was a strong chance that Angus Haws was waiting in the shelter of that cave, concealed, immune to attack from above or below, commanding a view of what lay below him in the pines.

And Jaine was there.

Anger shook Ter Bryant. Haws had judged right. He *had* to go back into that woods. He *had* to find Jaine. He *had* to know what threatened her, even though it meant walking into the trap Haws had set for him.

THREE

She was suspended in midair, her feet perhaps six feet above ground—less than that above the protruding, sharply pointed stakes that waited below. Her arms were extended, almost forming a cross. Rawhide thongs attached to her wrists reached toward cut branches in the trees on either side. The weight of her body had jerked her arms high and taut. Her body swayed slightly, hanging limp from her painfully extended shoulder sockets. Her head also hung down. Bryant, seeing her that way after more than a year's separation, felt the hot sting of tears. He could not tell if she was conscious.

But she had been, moments earlier. She had cried out in pain.

Jaine! Look up, hon'. Look up.

As if responding to his thought she raised her head slowly. A shock wave shivered through him. He saw the sweet face he remembered, but it was different in ways he could not have been prepared for. Her cheeks and jawline were leaner, somehow more prominent. Her skin was weathered to a deep tan. Her mouth was firmer, the tight-pressed lips showing strain. Her lovely gray eyes were dark with pain. What Ter Bryant saw was the difference between a girl's and a woman's face.

He took an involuntary step forward. The

movement caught her eye. Her whole body jerked taut. "Ter!" The cry rang with clear joy. Alarm followed instantly. "Stay back—he's behind me in those cliffs. Don't come near!"

The warning stopped Bryant while he was still in the cover of trees thirty yards east of her. His gaze shot past her toward the bluffs another fifty yards beyond. The cave whose ledge he had glimpsed was invisible now behind a curtain of tall pines, but he judged that it must be almost in a line with Jaine from his position.

He eased back, examining Angus Haws's trap more closely. As he took it in, anger burned stronger.

The trees grew thinner in places here. Jaine hung over what was in effect a cleared strip. There was no way to reach her from the front or the sides, where the undergrowth was light, without exposing himself to Haws, hiding in his cave beyond. The thongs by which Jaine's arms were attached to the smooth, peeled branches would be green, Bryant realized, and thoroughly wet down before they were used, causing the leather to stretch from her weight. As the rawhide dried—and the sun climbing overhead was already warm—it would begin to shrink. The cut branches would be pulled downward under increasing pressure. As soon as they came horizontal, perhaps before, the ends of the thongs would creep toward the tips of those branches.

Ter Bryant couldn't guess how long that would take. A half-hour. An hour. Perhaps several hours. And if Jaine survived that long ordeal on Angus Haws's cruel rack, as soon as the thongs jumped free of the high branches under the tightening pull, she would drop down upon the upraised stakes.

He couldn't let that happen. He couldn't wait, gambling on his ability to smoke Haws out in time. He had to try to free Jaine, just as Haws had planned. And when he did, the mountain man would get a clear shot at him. Bryant did not delude himself that Haws would need more than one.

It was simple and obvious, and Bryant could see no way out of it.

"Go back, Ter," Jaine called out. Her voice was low, the ring of joy no longer there. But there was something else that moved Ter Bryant even more, a helpless longing, the pain of love. "Leave us. He'll kill you. There's nothing you can do."

Bryant said nothing, in that moment unable to answer.

"Please. I couldn't bear it if . . . if that happened. If you leave he won't harm me."

Would that work? Could he pretend to leave, and trick Haws into releasing her?

Almost immediately Bryant saw that any such hope was an illusion. Haws wouldn't act until he was certain that Bryant had left the valley. Even that delay would jeopardize Jaine's life. Not even Haws could know for certain how long it would be before the drying thongs jerked free.

And what would be gained if he really left and Haws acted in time? He would only have to invade the valley again.

Suddenly Jaine began to twist violently, as if she were trying to force the thin leather strips to pull toward the ends of the smooth branches from which she hung.

"No!" Bryant yelled. "Jaine, don't!"

In panic he lifted his long rifle to his shoulder. If he could hit one of those thongs . . . no, the stakes below were too cunningly spaced, extending across the open strip beneath her. Even if she fell to one side, still in the grip of one of her bonds, she would be impaled on those sticks.

But if she fell outward, either forward or back . . .

"Swing!" he shouted suddenly. "Jaine, hon', swing out!"

She stopped twisting her body. She stared toward him, seeing a figure in leather thirty yards away, hardly visible at all in the shadowed undergrowth at the edge of the woods.

He realized that she hadn't understood. "Remember that swing on the big oak behind your house? The one you used to swing on? Can you swing out like that?"

He would have to step out into the clear to be

certain of the shot, to reduce the angle and lessen the risk of hitting her moving body. Could he hit a narrow strip of leather at thirty yards with one shot? He knew he wouldn't get another. And he would have to time the shot when Jaine was at the end of her outward swing to be certain that the remaining attached length of rope wouldn't pull her down onto the row of stakes. It seemed like a long gamble, involving certain exposure to Angus Haws's fire, but Bryant saw that he had to take it.

"That's it," he urged as Jaine began to respond, understanding what he wanted, straining to set her body into motion. "Try harder. Hurry, hon'! Trust me!"

Haws wouldn't give them much time. Might he even act against Jaine rather than see her freed? Bryant shook off that fear. There was no other way. Already, under the increasing pressure of Jaine's struggles as she forced her body into a pendulum swing backward and forward, the leather ends attached to the high branches seemed to have slipped closer to the tips.

His rifle was primed and ready to fire. It was a Kentucky rifle he had purchased from William Bent after losing his favorite old Hawken in the desert scrape with Comanches. He felt surer of his aim when he could rest the long barrel of the Kentucky rifle on something, but here that wouldn't be possible. His hands were sweating and he wiped them on his thighs. Damn! They were shaking, too. Would they cost him his aim? At twelve years of age he had hit targets no bigger at twice this range and more, but no such burden had weighed upon him then. Now he felt the weight and pressure of his long search all gathered into a single moment. Jaine's life—and his—rode on a single shot.

She was swinging freely now, back and forth, the arc lengthening slightly with each swing, carrying her beyond the sharpened teeth of the stakes below. *Once more, hon'*, he breathed. *Now another. Yes . . .*

He stepped into the clear and dropped to one knee, in the same movement bringing his rifle to his shoulder.

FOUR

Lying prone on the ledge at the front of the cave, Angus Haws was hidden from Ter Bryant's view, but he had a clear window in the screen of pine branches through which he could see Willow suspended above the clearing.

When Bryant first called out to her, Haws couldn't see him. After a few minutes peering toward the woods at the far end of the cleared strip he made out what might have been a deer. It didn't move. Haws sighted on that patch of brown, then slowly lowered his rifle. He couldn't be certain of such a shot. He couldn't see the man's head, or even be sure of hitting him in the chest or belly.

He would wait. Bryant would come into the open soon.

Willow's joyful cry of recognition angered him. Then he heard her successively warning Bryant and pleading with him to leave, saving himself, and Haws's anger became a bitter, jealous rage. For a while that fury seemed almost savage enough to drive him from his hidden perch down into the forest. He could kill Bryant as easily there, and the hot pleasure of the thought nearly overrode reason.

In the end his boiling passion subsided enough for his trapper's instinct to prevail. The certain catch was better. What if Willow cried for joy when she saw her dandy? What if she wept when he died? Those tears would dry.

Bryant spoke to her. Angus Haws heard the urgency in his voice but he couldn't make out the words. Scowling, he watched Willow. She appeared to be listening intently, waiting for something. What could Bryant do? He couldn't reach her through the woods from either side, for the growth was thin enough there, as Haws had determined before he set his trap, to give him an easy shot. What was he up to?

Now Willow was struggling. She lifted her legs

and thrust forward, using the surprising strength in that slender body. Haws's scowl deepened. She would pull one of those cords loose if she didn't stop, and plummet onto the stakes below. That was a chance Haws had risked, but he didn't expect it to happen, didn't want it. Bryant called out again encouragingly. He was less than a hundred yards away. Perhaps eighty, eighty-five yards. Haws's rifle lifted again.

Suddenly he understood the reason for Willow's actions. Anger returned in a rush. He took quick aim at the patch of brown in the woods at the far end of the clearing.

Then the man moved. In one leap he emerged from the trees into the open. Haws's anger turned to exulting satisfaction. Bryant dropped to his knee, lifting his rifle. Angus Haws swung the muzzle of his toward the open target.

He stiffened.

The woman was directly between them. The man's shift of position had placed him in direct line with Willow. Because Haws was on the higher ledge, Willow hanging from the trees, the man Bryant kneeling on the ground beyond her, the angle was such that her swinging body blocked his line of fire. Only at the bottom of her swinging arc was Bryant briefly visible above her.

Damn her, then! Let her take the bullet if she must!

Haws took dead aim at the man, waiting for the swing of the woman's body, his finger crooked over the trigger.

He didn't shoot. There was sweat on his face. His heart pounded. He hardly understood the weakness that would not let him squeeze the trigger in careless disregard for Willow's life.

From eighty yards away came the crack of a rifle shot. Haws ducked instinctively. Then he lifted his head, knowing Bryant couldn't see him. His gaze darted toward Willow.

She continued to swing back and forth. The branches from which she hung jerked as she hit the bottom of her arc. But nothing happened. Bryant had missed!

Teeth bared in satisfaction, Angus Haws rose to his hands and knees and scuttled swiftly along the ledge, searching for another opening in the branches before him, a window that would give him a different angle and a clear shot at the man on the ground.

Haws knew that *he* wouldn't miss.

FIVE

Ter Bryant's brain seemed to be frozen, turned into ice by the shock of his missed shot. Somehow his body continued to function. He shook powder from his horn and poured it down the long barrel of the Kentucky rifle. A lead ball followed it smoothly, then a greased patch, the motions proceeding without thought, executed with swift precision.

All the while, he waited for the impact of Angus Haws's bullet smashing into his body. Why hadn't it come? The puzzling question unnerved him almost as much as his failure to hit one of the thongs from which Jaine swung with his first shot. *Why hadn't Haws shot him down?*

He raised the long, heavy barrel once more, squinting to bring the slender strip of rawhide attached to Jaine's left wrist into view.

A blur of movement tugged at the corner of his vision.

His gaze lifted. In that instant he saw Angus Haws for the first time through a small gap in the wall of pines in front of the bluffs. Haws was crawling along a ledge. He stopped, looking up, his full beard distinctly visible.

Without conscious decision Ter Bryant tipped the muzzle of his rifle from right to left, quickly sighting on the distant ledge, catching Haws in his sights almost immediately as the trapper lifted his head. The calculations Bryant made in his head for height, wind and distance were automatic, reflexive, the decisions of a man to whom shooting a rifle had become a habit of long years. He had missed a smaller target once. He would not miss again.

There was no hesitation between the moment he caught Angus Haws in his sights and the smooth squeeze of the trigger.

Haws reared up on his knees. The smell of powder stung Bryant's nostrils as he saw the huge body pitch forward. It teetered on the edge of the ledge. Then Haws dropped out of sight, plunging toward the bottom of the cliffs.

Having climbed one of the pines and loosened its length of rawhide thong, with shaking hands Ter Bryant lowered Jaine toward the ground. He had to lean far out, hanging onto the cut branch with one hand, making his arms' reach an extension of the cord, until Jaine's feet dropped below and in front of the row of pointed stakes.

He released the leather. Jaine crumpled to the ground.

In panic Bryant skinned down the tree. As he jumped to her side she was already lifting her head, holding out her arms. A smile trembled on her lips. "I'm sorry, Ter," she said. "My legs . . . I guess I'm just weak. I couldn't stand up."

Grinning with relief, he took her into his arms, lifting her from the ground. He held her tightly, his heart too full for speech. Her cheek was wet, scraping against the black beard she had never seen before.

"It's over, hon'," he murmured. "It's over."

She drew back. Her eyes, brimming with tears,

were fixed upon his face almost shyly, with a kind of surprise, as if she couldn't believe who he was and what he had become. She reached up to touch his face.

Her glance went past him. He saw something flash in her eyes. Then she screamed.

SIX

Haws remembered the grizzly he'd killed at the finger lakes. He had put his first bullet into the great bear's heart, and still it had charged him.

Something inside Haws had broken loose. He could feel it flopping around. Bryant's bullet was lodged in his chest, high up. When he coughed there was blood. He could feel the weight of the lead ball, the thickness of it, like something caught in his throat. He could feel the looseness inside when he moved, like water sloshing in a pail. He could feel the life seeping out.

But he rose and staggered through the pine woods toward the man who had shot him. He had broken something else on the rocks at the bottom of the cliff. His left wrist was crooked. And he had lost his rifle in the fall. No matter. He had other weapons—his knife, his hatchet, his hands.

That grizzly hadn't even gone down from the

second bullet. He was some, that one. He'd just kept coming. As Haws kept moving, carrying the weight of the bullet.

The trees thinned out suddenly and he saw the man and the woman on the ground. He was lifting her up, holding her tightly. Haws felt a generalized anger. It was not so much a rage against the bullet in his chest or the woman as it was a rebellion against what was happening to him. He hadn't checked his traps again that morning. He knew he would never check them again. He would never slip naked into an icy stream, sniffing like a beaver for the scent of danger, never feel the sun hot on his back while he drifted in his dugout canoe, never ride lonely and silent along a wilderness trail. He couldn't see the high peaks any more. Everything was hazy beyond a very short range. He had a sense of something ending at last, something that never should have ended, that should have gone on forever.

He fumbled his hatchet from his belt. His anger rumbled loose in his chest, and he fixed his eyes on the man in the clearing as he charged.

Bryant ran for the long rifle he had leaned against a tree before he climbed. But Haws was too close. He couldn't reach it.

He took time to dart a look at Jaine to make sure she was out of the way. She stood rooted, paralyzed. But Haws was coming toward him, not Jaine.

Bryant thought of running. He saw blood on Haws's chest and hands, and he was charging on wobbly legs. He wouldn't last through much of a chase. But Bryant couldn't run. Something inside wouldn't let him. His hand closed on the hilt of his bowie knife as he jumped forward to meet the trapper's attack, threading through the lines of stakes Haws had planted.

The move surprised Angus Haws. Bryant saw the surprise in his bright blue eyes as Haws raised his ax and swung.

Bryant dodged, slashing out with his blade as Haws rode past him. He didn't come close. But Haws's wild swing of his hatchet also missed. And he couldn't stop. He just kept going, out of control, and then he was blundering into his own trap, unable to stop himself, plunging out of control and pitching forward, both arms flung out as if to break his fall. His huge body landed across the twin rows of stakes that pointed skyward like a bed of spears.

There was one last, explosive "Waugh!"

Then it was really over.

Books are produced in the United States using U.S.-based materials	Books are printed using a revolutionary new process called THINKtech™ that lowers energy usage by 70% and increases overall quality	Books are durable and flexible because of Smyth-sewing	Paper is sourced using environmentally responsible foresting methods and the paper is acid-free

Center Point Large Print
600 Brooks Road / PO Box 1
Thorndike, ME 04986-0001 USA

(207) 568-3717

US & Canada:
1 800 929-9108
www.centerpointlargeprint.com